Marshmallows

Louise Willingham

lost boys press

For Dan.

It's okay.

You are tenacious.

Tuesday, 7ᵗʰ of January
Early in the morning

One

I'm a mess.

It's warm and cosy in my little bed with Dan wrapped around me, but I wake up with a scream in my throat. Cool sweat is sticking to my back, and I can't stop shaking.

"I am here," he whispers.

But what if you weren't?

I don't want to be awake. Did I wake him up too? Annoyed with myself, I screw my eyes shut.

"William?"

I shove my face into the pillow and hide. Dan rubs his hand steadily into my back, giving me time to come back to reality. I appreciate it.

I'm not used to nightmares.

Dan gets them every night and he just sort of...goes back to sleep. How? I'm trapped in that memory of something I imagined.

I can't even remember the whole dream. The feeling

of helplessness lingers, though. As does the distinct lack of Daniel. It's like when he went to New Zealand, but twenty times worse.

"William?"

I wipe my eyes and twist awkwardly to look at him. He's as close to me as it's possible to get, and even in the darkness, I can tell he's frowning. His bright eyes reflect the weak light bouncing in from outside and I just start crying again.

Dan tuts softly and snuggles me into his chest, pulling the duvet right up to my ears so I'm hidden from the world. The arm I'm not pinning beneath the pillow wraps around my shoulders.

"I have you," he promises. "Talk when you're ready."

I want to be able to say *I'm okay* and just fall back asleep, but disjointed images of grey skies and pale skin keep flickering through my head. I put my hand on his warm waist, grounding myself, and take a slow breath. It tastes of Dan—of faint cigarettes and deodorant—and it helps.

"I don't know what it was," I begin. "I think the world was *different* somehow, and you'd gone away."

Dan lets out a little sigh. "I will have to leave for my VISA."

Ugh. "Yeah," I grumble, "I know. Maybe that was it—maybe I was thinking about it."

He kisses my hair again. "You know I will always come back."

The disbelieving sound in my throat makes him chuckle, and it's so reassuring that I feel some of the tension leave my shoulders.

"I *will*, darling."

Dan's VISA doesn't usually concern me. Even immediately after being hospitalised, he was able to work out the logistics of reapplying in order to keep studying. And he must have got it right because he's in bed with me right now. But that was for university. What about when he's no longer a student? It's not something we've ever really had a chance to talk about.

"When do you have to leave again?" I ask, flattening my hand against his back, like holding him tighter will keep him here forever.

Dan relaxes his arm and twists his fingers through the back of my hair instead of holding a handful of the duvet. He talks softly, trying to coax me back to sleep, and I resist for as long as possible.

"After re-sits," he whispers. "If I fail, I can reapply and start my third year again. If I graduate..."

No more student VISAs. I know this. I hate this. Unless he applies for a master's, which would require him to firstly find one he likes and secondly get good enough grades, the only way he'll be able to stay in the country is if he gets a job. A good job at that—something he'd have to prove to the UK government that he's absolutely perfect for.

Immigration is difficult.

I know he's terrified of this not working. I am too, and it must have been playing on my mind. All I can remember from my dream is the crushing fear of loneliness and an awareness that I was missing something important. I was missing Dan.

This is going to hurt.

Even if he only has to go to Russia for a few weeks. Even the best-case scenario is unpleasant.

I tighten my arm around him while he talks. Usually, the coaxing back to sleep is my job, but it turns out Dan is *very* good at it. His voice is quiet and I swear he sometimes shifts language, but I'm too close to unconsciousness to be sure.

Tuesday, 7ᵗʰ of January
When the sun is up

Two

Tuesday morning is cold and overcast. I cuddle to Dan for as long as he'll let me, but honestly, we need to move. We've been cramped together in my single bed since eleven last night when we got back from the social. When we got back from my coming out.

In my concern about Dan's VISA, I haven't really given myself chance to panic over the fact that my friends know I'm bisexual.

Bisexual. I keep running the word through my head, trying it on like a new shirt. It's a big word. A heavy word. But last night, it felt as safe as saying *Goodness, it's cold outside*.

Coming out to my friends went well—as well as I could have hoped. No one really seemed surprised, which is both relieving and concerning. Was I really that obvious?

Probably.

Dan gets dressed and goes to the communal kitchen to make coffee. His confidence now, compared to last week when we argued about being on campus together, is amazing. It's like he never worried about my flatmates speculating on my sexuality. It's like he never worried, even for a moment, that Matthew would find out about me.

This is the biggest difference us becoming *official* has made.

I get out of bed very slowly. Cold is seeping in despite the radiator and I don't relish the thought of being here on my own today. But I don't have a choice. My first exam is tomorrow and I absolutely need to revise.

The door opens again and Dan sneaks in, mug of coffee in one hand and glass of water in the other.

Oh, damn. I bet he wishes he were going outside for a cigarette.

I give him a big smile and take the glass. "Thanks," I say. "How are you?"

He sits beside me on the edge of the bed and reaches back to smooth the duvet out. "Good, thank you. Did you sleep better?"

Ugh. I'd managed to forget about my nightmare, but now the fear of him leaving and never returning is right at the front of my thoughts.

I lean sideways into him and nod.

"Do you want to talk more about it?"

"Nah." I sigh. "Just promise me that when you do go back we'll stay in touch."

Dan sighs and puts his free arm around me. "Naturally. It will not be for long. Even if I graduate, I will be back soon."

Obviously I want him to graduate. He deserves it. He's been working to keep up with his course reading, even though he isn't going to lectures. I think his brain works like mine: if we're not actively working on something, things go wrong. We spiral out of control. I lose the ability to do so much as washing up, and Dan... I dread to think what would happen to Dan if he were bored.

I put my arm around his back.

"I *should* graduate," he mutters. "And I should have a good guess at how I have done, which will help with job applications." He kisses my hair suddenly, like he's decided something. "I will keep my apartment."

"What if you're away for months?"

He grunts. He doesn't like that thought.

"You can keep the keys for me."

There's a suggestion just waiting to be whispered. I could live with him next year. He's closer to the hospital. It would be nicer than being in another year of university accommodation—or, even worse, trying to find a group of people to house share with.

"I'll keep them safe," I promise.

Dan kisses my hair again.

"Pop in every few days to make sure you haven't got rats or something."

He laughs and sits up straight to sip at his coffee. "Yeah," he says. "Good idea."

I leave the question mark surrounding our future hanging over us like a forgotten cobweb. We'll get to it one day. We'll work it out but, for now, it isn't a problem. Dan *will* get a job here—he just will. I can't afford to consider an alternative.

Dan stays with me until nine, when he leaves with a promise to phone me at five. We're both going to spend the day studying before I go to his flat for the night.

"We could go out for dinner," I blurt as Dan steps out into the cold morning air. It's a little strange that he isn't clicking a lighter and surrounding himself in smoke, but I don't comment on it. Why would I? He doesn't need reminding.

He reaches up to cup my chin with his fingertips. "Would you like that?"

The butterflies in my stomach make it difficult to say, "Yes."

"I think it would be nice," Dan whispers. "But you are working hard today, so it's okay if you change your mind."

I love him.

I grin, absolutely confident that I want to go out for a meal with my *boyfriend*, and nod. "Thanks. I'll let you know if I do, but I wanna do this."

Dan looks happy enough to cry. Instead, he leans down and presses a warm, sweet kiss to my cheek. It steals my breath and leaves me shivering.

"Have a good day, William," he murmurs. "I love you."

"Wait!" I grab the front of his jacket and stop him from stepping away. "I love you too. Have a good day and call me if you need anything, all right?"

Dan nods. His head is still bowed so our faces are close together, and then I kiss him.

His hand drops from my chin to hold my fingers very lightly. It's cute. I kiss him sweetly, smiling and making sure he has plenty of opportunities to move back, and let out a surprised little *oh* when he tugs me firmly into his chest.

"I am proud of you," he says, voice muffled by my hair. "I need to go. You need to work."

I groan, being overdramatic.

"William."

"*Fine.*"

I let him go.

Dan smiles at me like he's committing this moment to memory, steps back, and turns away.

I watch until he's around the corner and out of sight.

Three

Pen down, I snatch my phone up to check the timer. I've finished my practice exam paper with twenty minutes left to spare, and I lean back in my desk chair for a quick break before I start going through my answers.

11:18 Lilley: How are you? Are you celebrating Christmas together?

I stare at my phone for a long minute, confused. Have I somehow skipped backwards in time? It is *definitely* January. Christmas was *definitely* two weeks ago.

12:03 William: We're fine, thanks. Both studying and we're meeting up later. Christmas was weeks ago, Lil

12:06 Lilley: Christmas

in the UK was, yeah.
They celebrate it today
in Russia. TODAY, Will

I stare out of the window for a moment, wondering if I have the energy for this. It's a very cold day. The grass outside my window is more brown than green, and only an idiot would choose to spend time outside when they could be sitting less than a metre away from a radiator.

I phone Lilley.

"Hey," she says, cheerful and not at all like she just told me something life-changing.

I cut straight to it. "What the hell are you on about?"

Lilley snorts a laugh. "Will, you should know this. Your boyfriend is Russian."

My stomach does a little flip, but now isn't the time to think about how hearing her talk about *my boyfriend* makes me feel. I settle for a huge grin.

"How do *you* know?"

"Hi," Cassie says, making me jump. Apparently, I'm on speaker. "I was being nosy and looking into Russian traditions. Did you know they're really into fortune-telling? It's a *thing* over there, especially at Christmas."

"But why do they do it in January?" I ask. My neck feels tight, like I've pulled a muscle. "Why has no one ever mentioned this to me before?"

Cassie sighs. "It's to do with the calendar they use—"

"They use a different *calendar*?"

Lilley laughs, but I feel like I've been thrown out of the window. There is so much to Dan that I just don't know. Will I ever learn it all? Or am I going to be catching up for the rest of our relationship—for the rest of our life?

Because I don't see any end to our relationship.

That thought fills me with excited, nervous bubbles. I'm like a shaken bottle of champagne.

"Google it," Lilley suggests. "Maybe you could get him a card or something. You said you're meeting later, right?"

I grind my teeth. "Right."

"I'm sure he'd love it if you got him a card. Just something to say you know and acknowledge that if he was at home—"

"Sure, Lilley, like I could give my *boyfriend* a Christmas card if he was in Russia!"

She sighs sharply. I probably deserve it, but a tight line of stress is tugging across my forehead. What should I do? How am I supposed to make this perfect? It needs to be perfect. After the start to the year Dan's had, I need to make this memorable for the *right* reasons.

Lilley seems to agree. "Then make the most out of the opportunity you've got, dumbass."

I rush through marking my practice exam, reasoning it's something I can focus more on tonight when I'm at Daniel's flat, and slam my pen down on the desk. I haven't focused at all in the half hour since talking to Lilley and Cassie, far too preoccupied with trying to work out how to make today special.

If anyone asks—if, by some chance, I see Peter—I'll tell them I'm having a break for lunch.

Not like I have time to eat today.

I pull on my coat and shoes, check my wallet, keys, phone, and head out. The sky is even darker than earlier, and I shove my hands into my pockets, trying to keep warm.

Buses leave from campus every ten minutes, so it isn't long until I'm sitting on an uncomfortable, rickety chair on a smelly, slightly crowded bus.

I'm not sure I've thought this through.

Maybe this is just going to upset Dan. Maybe he didn't mention it for a reason. It's not like he ever tries to bring his culture into our day-to-day life, so why would he want to be reminded about the country he's trying so hard to leave behind?

The bus rattles down the hill towards the town centre, and I kind of regret not bringing my revision notes with me. The journey is longer than I thought, and not having flashcards makes me feel guilty. But this isn't wasted time.

I spend the whole journey doubting myself and Googling Russian Christmas traditions.

How am I going to do this? Will anywhere still be selling cards a week into January? Bloody hell. What am I doing?

I hop off the bus at the station, stomach twisting a little

bit from reading while travelling. It's raining now—it must be slightly too warm for snow, which is a huge disappointment—and I haven't brought any shopping bags. Great. It feels like a bad omen, and I consider turning on the spot and getting back on the bus.

Wilkinson's is the first shop on my right. Mum usually does half her Christmas preparation shopping there—things like wrapping paper and stocking fillers—so I put all my faith into it and dash through the rain towards the building. I splash straight through puddles, soaking my shoes, and tumble through the sliding doors.

My heart sinks. It looks like the shop has thoroughly moved past Christmas and even New Year's. The aisles are lined with yellow packets of mini eggs and bottles of antibacterial cleaning products advertising sweet, floral scents. Not a Christmas wreath in sight.

Oh, God.

My stomach rumbles but I ignore it, searching each aisle until I come to a very sad, very chaotic *reduction* section. Amongst the mess, there's a packet of chocolate coins, some better-than-half-price tinsel, and a Christmas card with a dog-eared corner without an envelope.

I take all three and almost burst into hysterical laughter when the cashier stares at my could-have-been-festive bundle.

"Bit late for Christmas shopping," he says.

Tell me about it. "It's Christmas *today* in Russia," I say. But I need to explain myself. The cashier looks at me like I just told him I'm buying a Christmas card as an Easter gift.

"My—my friend is Russian. I'm getting him this as a surprise, but he didn't give me any warning."

Friend.

My cheeks burn red with shame. *Boyfriend. Boyfriend.*

Why couldn't I have just said *boyfriend*?

"That's so cool," the cashier says, scanning the card. It comes up as thirty pence, which I think is pushing it. "I guess he's a student at the uni, right?"

I nod and freeze, like someone just clamped their hand over my mouth. What am I thinking? How many Russian boys are there in Stoke? How many go to Keele University?

What are the chances that this cashier knows Matthew? What are the chances that I just ruined everything?

"I'm starting there in September," he says, cheeks pinching pink. Maybe I've scared him with my expression, but I can't think past the memory of last Friday. Images flash through my mind, one after another, like stills from a movie.

"Danny!"

Dan's cold, clammy hand taking mine. The irregular sound of our frightened footsteps as we ran away from Matthew, clinging to each other.

The cut on Dan's eyebrow which has since melted into a sprawling green and yellow bruise—

"Are you studying there?" the cashier asks.

I blink. "Yeah." Would this guy know Matthew if he isn't a student yet? I've overreacted. Like always. "Medicine."

I've definitely overreacted.

The cashier smiles at me, pink cheeks burning to red, and throws a glance again at the card I've bought. "Medicine? That's amazing."

I shrug. "I guess."

Fortunately for us, someone joins the queue behind me. What a relief. I beep my card, throw a smile at the cashier, thank him, and bundle up my crumpled purchases.

It's still raining. I didn't think about that. Bloody hell.

I stuff the chocolate into my pocket and cuddle the card and tinsel under my coat and make a run for it. I think I'm going to get straight on a bus, but instead I go down the hill to the high street, splashing in yet more puddles.

I can't just give Dan a crumpled card for Christmas. He deserves more.

I bet he thought he'd got out of this when he was out of the country for the twenty-fifth of December. Part of me worries, again, that he's not going to like this reminder of Russia. It's not like he's ever shared *good* memories of the place. He doesn't sit and reminisce over things he used to do and people he used to know.

But how much of that is him just not trusting that he's safe? I know Matthew never wanted him to talk about his life before uni.

Maybe I should ask. Or let him know that I understand today is significant.

I duck out of the rain and find myself in a cheap "we sell everything" sort of shop. Right in front of me is a crate of reduced-price Christmas puddings, each in battered cardboard boxes and looking decidedly unappetising. Something about Dan makes me think he's the sort of person to love Christmas pudding so, even though I can't stand it, I grab one.

I also grab a reusable shopping bag and make sure my receipt from Wilkinson's is easy to access, should anyone question the sad tinsel cradled within my coat.

I wish I could give Dan a proper gift, but what would I buy him? Almost everything in his flat is brand new.

I pace the aisles, searching for anything that might make Dan smile. In the grocery section, I find a bag of ground coffee claiming to be a Christmas edition. Caffeine is Dan's final addiction, and not one I'm particularly eager to break him from.

The coffee joins the pudding and shopping bag in my basket.

I'm beginning to think this will have to be enough, but a severely reduced and damaged fake tree catches my eye near the checkout. It's one foot tall, including the stand and long stick at the top. Tiny. Perfect.

I add it to the basket.

Now that I've got a tree, I need decorations. The tinsel I bought is far too big for this job, so I go in and out of a few more shops before finding a gaudy pink and green set of one-inch baubles. I don't like them. They definitely won't go with the dark, classy colour scheme in Dan's flat but I don't really care. They will have to do.

It's a pathetic little attempt at Christmas but I think it's good enough. I think Dan will appreciate it. I hope it's a *good* surprise.

Four

Two very familiar people catch my eye as I hurry back to the bus station. Lilley, dressed in a practical black waterproof that comes down to her knees, and Cassie, dressed in a much less practical bubble-gum pink puffer jacket that looks like it's absorbing more rain than it's repelling.

I see them together and my heart skips.

I'm saved the difficulty of deciding whether to say *hi*, because Cas sees me and waves her arm in the air like she's signalling a jet.

I clutch the shopping bag close and splash over to them. We duck under the shelter of an overhang outside a row of shops and laugh at each other, cold rain dripping from our noses.

"Thought you were busy studying," Lilley says, clinging to Cassie's hand. To her *girlfriend's* hand.

I grin so much it hurts.

"Quick break to do some incredibly *last-minute* shopping," I say, lifting the bag an inch or so. "It's not much, but—"

"What have you got?" Cas asks, snatching the bag from me. They open it between them and peer through the pathetic contents. "Okay, this is cute."

"Where did you find the tree?" Lilley laughs, looking at me through her eyelashes. "This must be the first Christmas tree bought this year."

I roll my eyes. "Cheap shop down the hill," I say. "Do you think it's okay?"

"Bit of a miserable attempt at Christmas, if I'm honest." Lilley sighs. My heart sinks. "But yeah. You've done well for a week into January."

"Dan's gonna love it," Cassie says, trying to hand me the bag back.

Lilley keeps hold of it. She isn't done being nosy.

"Is he?" I mutter. "I'm not sure."

Cassie frowns. "Why not?"

"It's a reminder of everything he's trying to leave behind, isn't it?"

Lilley takes the bag from Cas and rummages through.

"Christmas is *nice*, though," Cassie presses. "A time for family and stuff."

I shrug. "Dan's mum was Spanish, and his dad fucked off when he was a teenager. I don't think he's that bothered about *family*."

Cassie forces her mouth into a tight line and hums, like she's beginning to doubt this idea too.

Ah, damn. If even Cas is having second thoughts about this, maybe I've really messed up.

Lilley finally looks up from the bag, eyes sharp and critical. "You haven't got any lights for the tree."

"Lil, I've barely got a tree!"

She sniggers and finally lets me reclaim my shopping. "You said it. In a rush to get back? We were just going to grab coffee."

I guess I could sit with them for half an hour.

I regret agreeing as soon as I nod, but I follow them back through the rain and through the glass doors of a café. The wooden floor is soaked and slippery, so we very carefully make our way over to the counter.

Lilley and Cassie both grab sandwiches, but I'm suddenly so aware that I should be revising that I can't stomach the thought of eating.

Lil stares at me like a disapproving mother. "You need fuel."

"I do, but I've got leftover soup for when I get home," I say, lying through my teeth. I haven't thought about eating today and I *know* I should take this opportunity to get some lunch but...I can't.

I don't want to eat right now. I'm too nervous, and too stressed about the fact I should be busy with my revision notes. Plus, I don't like the look of any of the options.

Lil purses her lips. "Sandwich? Cake? I'll buy—"

"Don't you dare," I say. My head spins at the thought of eating a whole slice of cake and I lean into the counter, leaving a puddle where water drips from my coat. "I'm fine. I'll have hot chocolate—that will keep me going until soup."

This non-existent soup is doing a lot of heavy lifting this afternoon.

Lilley hums, not convinced. "Fine. I'm buying your drink though—"

"Lil—"

"Don't bother arguing." Cassie laughs. "You know what she's like."

"I do," I grumble.

So, I let Lilley buy me hot chocolate. She gets marshmallows on the top, so I guess that counts as food. Right?

God, I know it doesn't. I know I'm being stupid and stubborn, but even though this is a lovely few minutes with two of my favourite people, I can't help but feel like I'm doing the wrong thing. I should be on a bus by now, revising or checking my emails. I should be reading through the newest articles concerning methods of diagnosing diseases or brushing up on anatomy.

My phone is out and on the table in front of me. I've just opened a saved PDF when Lilley reaches out and snatches my phone away.

"Lil!"

"Ten minutes of your time, Will." She sighs, turning off the screen and keeping it hostage on their side of the table.

I bristle.

"Honestly. Give your eyes a rest."

I groan loudly and glare out of the window at the rainy

street, chewing the inside of my cheek. "I've already had an hour's break."

"Make it an hour and ten."

Fine. Making sure she can see that I'm pouting, I scoop the marshmallows from my hot chocolate with a teaspoon and pop them in my mouth. They're sickly sweet.

I'll eat something proper tonight when I'm with Dan. Promise.

"How was last night?" Cassie asks, peeling the crusts from her sandwich.

Lilley takes them wordlessly from her and I grin, amazed at how perfectly they already fit together.

"Lovely," I say, but it's a lie. My nightmare, and worrying about losing Dan for an indefinite length of time, was horrible and overshadowed the achievement of coming out. My expression drops. "It's always lovely to be with him," I correct.

Lilley smirks, not noticing that I changed my answer. "You're so romantic. It's disgusting."

"He needs it, Lil."

Cassie nods. "I hate to agree with Will—"

"Hey!"

"—but he's right. Dan *needs* adoring." Cassie shrugs. "The guy's a mess."

I won't deny that.

Lil grimaces. "He did look a bit of a mess on Friday, if I'm honest."

I nod. I don't want to be talking about this, but I guess we should. "Friday was a low point."

They share a look. I'm not certain, but I'm fairly confi-dent that Cas knows why Lilley and I were at the hospital on Friday. They got together Friday evening. Lilley *must* have explained her sudden and intense period to her best friend—to her girlfriend.

I'll have to check, though.

"Is it something you can tell us?" Lilley asks, sliding my phone back across the table. "Or would you rather not?"

I'd rather not. But Peter knows, so I imagine he's already told Cas *some* of what happened. I'm pretty sure Lilley's already guessed most of it—she was *there* for most of it. Still, I'd rather tell them myself. Get the details right.

"Matthew relapsed," I mutter. I'm glad I didn't let Lil waste money getting food for me, because my stomach feels like a rock. "Actually on New Year's, but we didn't find out until Thursday."

Cas grimaces. "Relapsed? Is this to do with what you told me?"

I nod, grateful that she's being subtle. She and Lilley clearly haven't talked in detail about this, and I'm glad. They both know that Dan is recovering from an addiction, but apparently neither of them have told the other.

I appreciate that.

"So, Dan obviously went to see him," I say, "because he felt like he should. And they argued, and Dan was a mess, and he's been struggling since."

"I'm not surprised." Lilley sighs. "Poor guy. I did think he was going to be sick on Friday."

I nod. "I think it was close." I take a deep, steadying breath and break the ice for them. "You both know he was taking heroin, right?"

I ask, even though I *know* I've told them.

They share a look.

"You knew?" Cassie asks, wiping a crumb from Lilley's chin. "When did he tell you?"

"Friday," Lil admits. "You?"

"Honestly?" Cassie blushes, cheeks turning pink to match her coat. "Months ago. But he just said it was drugs, nothing specific."

"Thanks for not telling each other," I say, fidgeting with the teaspoon. "I know you probably wanted to."

Cassie nods enthusiastically. "Yep. But I realised it's not my place."

Lilley winks at me and takes a sip of her coffee. "Same, hon."

For a moment, I compare them to Peter. I hate myself for doing it, but Cassie and Lilley have been perfect. A little pushy, yeah—but perfect. Peter, on the other hand...

Was an arse.

I keep telling myself I've forgiven him for how he behaved about Dan, but this bitterness in my chest suggests maybe not. I know Dan says he's okay with it all, but am I?

I'm not so sure.

I need to talk to Peter again. Maybe after the exams are over we'll actually spend a day together—maybe with Dan and Anthony there too. I think I'd like that.

I let out a long sigh and wonder if I could have eaten something after all. "Thank you."

"No problem." Cassie takes another bite and tilts her head, watching me. "Is Dan okay? Like, *okay*?"

Blood leaves my cheeks again. I stall. "What do you mean?"

"Like, with heroin."

He's fine. I'm certain he's doing fine. Nevertheless, my voice shakes when I say, "Yeah, he's okay. He has a prescription and that's really helping."

Cas nods sharply. "Good. So he didn't go cold-turkey?"

I shake my head so hard my glasses slide down my nose. "God, no. He—fucking hell." I'm going to have to tell them. "Y'know when he broke his ribs? He went to the hospital and they helped him. Therapy, replacement drugs, regular blood tests. You name it."

Lilley nods. "And he's keeping up with all of that, right?"

"Yep. He talks to his therapist every day and he spends more time with doctors than I do."

Cas heaves a sigh of relief. "Won't lie, Will, I've been worried about this."

"What do you mean? About what?"

"About you trying to save a drug addict."

I glare at her across the table. "Recovered," I whisper. "Or, at least, recovering. And I didn't try to save him. I just wanted to be in his life so he knew there was someone who cared."

"Very on-brand," Lil says. "And he clearly wanted you to be there. The way he looks at you, Will..." she trails off and shudders. I'm not sure how much of it is exaggeration and how much of it is from the cold. "He adores you. It's gross."

"What, grosser than you two sharing sandwiches?" I ask, smirking at the way Cassie's cheeks burn red.

Lil kicks me under the table.

"What's he on?" Cas asks, quickly changing the subject.

I roll my eyes, but of course she's interested. Between us—a med student, a bio chem student, and a forensics science student—of *course* we're comfortable talking about drug therapies.

"Buprenorphine," I say. "Know it?"

Cassie takes a bite of her sandwich and nods, thoughtful. "That's an opiate too, right?"

"Yeah."

"And it helps?"

"I think so," I sigh, "but I'm not sure. Mostly. He gets really bad headaches and totally fails to hide them. And he's—" I hesitate. "He's always running a temperature. Hot flushes, y'know? But he doesn't really talk about it."

Lilley rolls her eyes. "Of course not. *Men.*"

"Excuse me?"

"You're terrible at talking about health," Lilley says, hitting me with a glare. "Y'know, things like addictions or headaches or the fact you haven't eaten today."

I blush. "I'm gonna eat when I get home, Lil," I mutter. "I said."

"Yeah, and I know you."

Cassie elbows her gently. "We're just worried for you,

Will," she says. "You've had a stressful start to the year."

I snort a laugh. "Stressful? Just a bit. But I'm fine, Cas. Honestly."

They give me a matching glare and it's so nice to see them working so perfectly as a couple that I forget to be irritated.

I grin at them, take a purposefully big mouthful of hot chocolate, and the conversation drifts on.

"Seeing him tonight?" Cas asks, taking another bite of her sandwich. "For dinner?"

"Yeah, and he has no idea about *this*," I say, nudging the bag by my feet. "I'm not sure how to get it all set up."

Lilley scoffs. "You have one tiny tree and a box of baubles. You could *set up* while he takes a piss."

I narrow my eyes at her, but it's not a bad suggestion.

"You'll come up with something," Cas says. "Send us pictures."

I squirm. "Not sure I'll get a chance to take any, but okay."

"Are you going back to campus?" Cas asks suddenly, taking a big drink of her tea. "Because we're going to the library after this."

"Really?" I think Lilley went to the library twice in the whole of our first year, and my disbelief is evident. "I am, yeah. Got another practice exam to work through."

"And soup to eat," Lil says, eyeing me over the top of her mug.

I sigh. "Yes, and soup to eat."

"Stick around another ten and we'll get the bus back with you," Cassie says, as if I can really afford to waste another half hour of my day.

Hang it.

I *can* afford to spend another few minutes with my friends, especially when they're so clearly full of love for each other. Just being sat opposite them makes me feel warm. I fight down the anxiety in me that's screaming *you should be studying*, and smile.

"Sounds good to me."

"Awesome." Lilley puts her mug back down and relaxes.

I sigh and glance out of the window before speaking again. It's still miserable out there, and I blame the rain for some of my grumpiness.

"How are you two?" I ask. "Clearly you're happy, but tell me more."

For once, Lilley's the one blushing. I could get used to this. Her green eyes sparkle and she looks sideways at Cas, as if she wants her girlfriend to answer for her.

Cas has always been pretty good at picking up subtle hints.

"I went to Lilley's on Friday night," she says. "First time we'd actually relaxed around each other in ages, and I ended up staying over. And—"

"I told her," Lilley says, grabbing Cassie's hand. "Both of you know about the abortion."

I nod, feeling my pulse tremble in my throat. "I told Dan."

Lilley rolls her eyes. "Like he couldn't work it out himself. That's fine—I just don't want you both telling *everyone*, because frankly, it's no one's business."

"I promise," I say gently. It dawns on me that, for once, Lilley is the vulnerable one. I don't like it. I feel like the world has been twisted the wrong way. "How *are* you?"

Lilley raises a dark eyebrow at me. "I'm fine, Will."

"Better than Friday night and Saturday," Cas adds.

Realising she's the one most likely to actually tell me what happened, I look at her.

"You don't have to pretend it didn't hurt," Cas continues, stroking the back of Lilley's hand. "Will—"

"Will *knows* it hurt," Lilley mutters. She won't look at either of us. "I threw up on him."

"Almost," I correct. "But yeah. I'm glad you're doing okay. Tell me more about *you two*."

Cas laughs and tucks some hair behind her ear. "Really?"

I shrug. "All I do is talk about Dan."

"True."

"I don't know what there is to say," Cas says, cheeks a rosy pink. "We cuddled, kissed, admitted we've been in love with each other for months, kissed some more."

I grin at them. They make it sound so easy. "I love that for you both."

Cas looks like the luckiest woman on Earth. I think she probably is. "Thanks, hon."

"Cas has been very patient with me," Lilley says softly. "I've been a pain in the ass."

And, as easily as breathing, they lean towards each other and kiss. My heartbeat thunders and I can't look away from them, stunned by their bravery, but I also don't want to see this. Why did I call Dan my *friend*? Why am I still finding it so impossible to be openly queer?

As quickly as they started, Lilley and Cas pull apart. In reality, their kiss lasted barely two seconds. It was a tiny, insignificant event in a café where hundreds of tiny, insignificant events happen each and every day.

But I value it so highly.

I grin at them both. "I'm so happy for you," I whisper. "I love this. I'm so proud."

Cas winks. "Your ex-girlfriend is a great kisser."

I cough an embarrassed laugh. "I know."

Lilley accepts the praise gratefully and gets back to her coffee. "Thanks. Now, Will, tell us about this revision we're keeping you from."

My hand twitches towards my phone. "Why?"

"It will help you feel like you're being productive, stupid," Lilley says. "And I'm interested. You have some cool ones, right?"

I pull a face. "Cool exams?"

"Like, one-on-one."

"Oh, yeah." I take another sip of my hot chocolate and launch into telling them about the different sorts of exams I have for my second year. They're all to prepare me for going into placements this semester, and include me having to interview an invigilator as if they're a patient. Saying I'm nervous about this is an understatement.

"Practice on us now," Lilley says, when far more than ten minutes have passed. "I'll tell you some symptoms and you—"

"It's not that easy," I say, panicking ever so slightly. What if I get it wrong?

Lilley waves my worries away with her hand. "Try anyway. Okay, so say I come hobbling in and I've got a really bad pain in my knees and it's been going on for months—"

"This doesn't work," I say quickly. "I know you, so I know—"

She touches her finger to her lips, shushing me. "Pretend."

Cassie tucks her hair behind her ears and laughs, doe eyes fixed on Lilley. Embarrassment twists in my stomach. Maybe this will give me a chance to talk through some of the methods I've been reading about for the last week.

We do get the bus together. Cassie and Lilley leave me by the library with two big hugs and I don't feel bad. I actually feel okay.

By the time I get to my room, a little soggy from the rain but otherwise happy, it's two. I'm meeting Dan at six. This gives me enough time to write his card and throw myself back into revision, starting by making flashcards for the paper I read on the bus and ending with another anatomy paper.

I carefully stash Dan's Christmas gifts behind my bed where they're out of view and not causing a distraction. I've had more than enough distractions this afternoon.

Five

My phone rings at exactly five o'clock. The highlighter I'm using on this old marking scheme slips and scrawls an obnoxious, yellow line across the page.

Never mind.

I see the caller ID and grin so much it lifts my glasses away from the bridge of my nose.

"Hey," I say, pen safely down.

"Привет," Dan whispers, sending icy cold shivers right through me. Speaking Russian must be a sign that he's not going to be *upset* about my Christmas surprise, right? It's not like months ago, when he was hurting so badly from Matthew that he barely even spoke to me out of fear I'd dislike his accent. "How are you doing?"

"Just finishing marking," I say, popping the cap back on the highlighter single-handedly. "You?"

"I am *bored*," he admits, dragging out the last word. "Have you done enough today?"

I will never forget how warm this makes me feel. Dan wants me to go to him. He's lonely and bored of working and he wants *me*.

I want him too.

"Definitely," I say, spinning in my chair so I'm facing away from my desk. I need to pack a bag. "Shall I come over? We could walk into town together for dinner."

"Is that okay?"

"Absolutely." I laugh. "I'll stay tonight and then we can come back here in the morning."

"Are you sure you want to stay with me?" Dan asks. "I know you are nervous about your exam."

I roll my eyes. "What, you think I'll sleep better while I'm missing you?" Doubt makes me freeze. "Unless you don't want me—"

"I do."

I blow raspberries. "Stop being so silly. I'll see you in half an hour, okay?"

"Okay. Я тебя люблю."

I grin at my bedroom. "I love you too, Dan."

I love him.

We hang up and the fact I can tell him this now—the fact he *knows*—almost makes me cry. That's the first time we've said it on the phone.

It's not the first time he's said it in Russian. He whispered it to me on Sunday night, when I'd decided to tell my friends about us. When I decided to come out to them all.

This Christmas thing is a good idea.

First, I phone for a taxi. This gives me fifteen minutes to get ready. I put some clean clothes into my bag with my wash kit and pack another bag with the Christmas gifts, wondering if I can hide them from Dan.

He's nosy. He's quick. He'll realise I'm hiding something in about three seconds.

Damn it.

I put my coat on, check I've got everything, and leave my room. It's always so much nicer waking up in Daniel's flat, but I do need to be on campus tomorrow.

For my exam. Oh, God.

My first-year exams were tough, but I know they were a breeze compared to what I'm expected to know for my second year. I've been working almost constantly for months and I'm confident that I remember everything I need to, yeah, but the exams are *intense*. There are two written ones, two lab-based exams, and the two interview-slash-consultation exams. I have a feeling they're going to be harder to diagnose than Lilley and Cassie.

I read through another article on the journey, risking travel sickness, and the taxi pulls up outside Dan's building just before I get to the conclusion. That's fine. I'll ask Dan to read it to me.

I pay the driver and tumble out with both of my bags. It's stopped raining, but the sky is heavy and dark. I don't tell Dan, but I get the distinct feeling it's going to snow.

He won't like that at all.

I text him to say I'm here and have just put my phone away

when the door swings open and he's there, looking heartbreakingly perfect in an evergreen jumper with sleeves rolled up to his elbows. The dark ink of his tattoo looks soft on his New Zealand-sun tanned skin, and I smile at it for a moment before remembering we have to speak.

"Hey," I say. "You look beautiful."

Dan's cheeks burn to a sunset red. Something deep within me lurches but I'm familiar enough with this feeling now to recognise it as *love*. God, I love him. I love the way he grins and looks down, embarrassed but sort of pleased about it. I love the way he hangs on to the doorframe, stopping himself from walking out into the puddles to meet me. He hasn't put shoes on yet.

"Are you nearly ready to go to dinner?" I ask, stepping right up to him.

He reaches for my bags before answering and I only let him take the one with my clothes. He frowns.

"Yes. But we don't have to rush."

I shrug. "Haven't eaten yet."

"*What*?"

I shrug again, hoping to convince him this isn't a big deal. "I was busy."

Dan has had enough days with me forgetting to eat now to not be surprised by this. Instead, he just groans and puts his arm around me as we climb the stairs together.

"I should have phoned you at lunch," he grumbles. "Oh, William. Are you hungry now?"

"Very."

He laughs, sounding relieved, and lets us into his flat. It always feels like coming home, even though he's only lived here a few months. We're only dropping off my bags and letting him fetch his coat and shoes, so I don't have time to settle down, but I relax.

I know how the settee feels and how the fabric smells. I know the sound the bathroom door makes when it squeaks on its hinges. I know how long it takes for the shower to heat up, and that there's a squeaky board under the carpet in his bedroom.

"Can I shove all this in your room?" I ask, waving the bag. "And then we can go straight out."

"Sure." Dan kisses my hair and leads the way, taking my clothes bag.

Inspiration.

"I'll get changed before we go," I say. "You look lovely. You're gonna outshine me."

Dan starts to complain, but I grin up at him, take the bag, and shove him back into the living room. I slam the door between us.

"Hey!"

"One minute!"

That has *definitely* made him suspicious. I've never kicked him out while I get changed before—certainly not for something as modest as a shirt.

I *will* change my shirt. First, I need to do some speedy decorating.

I take the tree out of my bag and fluff it, so the branches

aren't squashed. I put the baubles on haphazardly, drape the tinsel across the headboard, and put his card, pudding, coins, and coffee beside the tree on his bedside table.

It's a little bit pathetic, but it's also incredibly cute. I take a photo to send to Lilley, Cas, and Peter, knowing Lilley will have spread the message about today being Christmas. I wonder if any of them have messaged Dan about it.

"William!" Dan whines, clearly speaking with his head against the door. "Are you okay?"

I roll my eyes and pull my shirt over my head. "Yep! One minute!" I packed a spare jumper just in case he'd got himself looking smart, but I'm embarrassed to report that we're now both in green.

I can't ask him to change. That would mean coming into his bedroom, which would mean seeing the Christmas gifts, which would ruin the surprise. And make us late for going out to dinner.

We're gonna have to match.

I pull my coat back on, hiding the jumper from sight, and start towards the door. I double back and grab my glasses.

I keep considering contacts, but if one falls out and I lose it while I'm on a placement I'll be screwed.

I open the door and Dan's right there, hands gripping the doorframe. He has a cute, worried expression on his face, pulling his eyebrows together, and I reach up to cup his cheek while dragging the door shut behind me. I hope he didn't see.

"Time to go," I say, shunting him backwards.

"What are you hiding?" he mutters, suspicion making

him tense.

Well, there it is. I knew he'd notice. Fortunately, I have the *I haven't eaten* card and we really do need to get out soon if we want to make sure we get a table somewhere.

"Never you mind," I say, grinning and hoping he realises this thing I'm hiding is a *good* thing. "Let's go and get me fed."

Dan holds my waist and studies me for a moment. His bright blue eyes take my breath away, and I almost ruin the secret right there. "Tell me when we get back?"

Oh, absolutely. I grin up at him and kiss his chin, taking the opportunity to inhale deeply and take in the scent of his aftershave.

He smells like a miracle.

There's no trace of cigarette smoke on him now. There's nothing getting between me and the smell of Dan, and I can really appreciate him. He's sweet. He's warm. I could breathe him in all night.

Despite my eagerness to get us back outside, I've paused. Dan seems to realise I need a quiet moment and loops his arms around me, pulling me into the safety of his chest.

I don't think I could love him more if I tried. He bows down to rest his chin on my shoulder, breathing softly into my ear. Every moment I've had with Dan since he got back from New Zealand has been precious, but tonight feels significant.

Not just because we're wearing matching jumpers.

"Are you okay to walk?" he asks eventually, rubbing his hand in gentle circles against my lower back.

Into his chest, where he can't see, I roll my eyes. "Yes,

Daniel. I could do with the exercise actually." Not like I didn't spend the afternoon running through the rain. "Barely moved all day."

It works. Dan groans into my neck and mutters, telling me I need to look after myself more.

"But you do such a good job of looking after me already," I whisper.

Dan stands up and hits me with another one of his *don't be dense, please* glares. A laugh snorts out of me and the quiet moment is over. I don't mind, because I know he'll always find the time to stop everything and hold me, but I wish I'd taken the opportunity to kiss him rather than laugh. He's so rarely within reach.

Standing at his full height, Dan is a foot taller than me. The best thing about this is how cosy I feel when we hug. The very worst thing is that I can't peck him on his cheek whenever I want.

I take his hand and kiss his knuckles instead. His wrists barely look damaged now, but knowing that he hurt himself just four days ago makes me queasy. I'm stealing glances at each of his wounds at every opportunity, but I've been doing that since we met. The cut and bruise across his eyebrow are less horrible than yesterday.

His wrists are my main concern at the moment. Months ago it was his knuckles, then his ribs. This is a different fear. Holding the hand of someone you know has the capacity to cause themself pain sets off a unique sort of survival instinct, and everything in me is poised to protect him. I wish I could hear his thoughts or, slightly more practically, hold on to him every second of every day.

I'm not very subtle about it. I hover near him while he pulls on his shoes, lacing them tight and neat. He lets go of me for a moment while he puts his coat on. As we walk down the stairs, Dan frees his hand again and shoves both of his coat sleeves up. We pause just inside the front door.

"Look." He sighs, holding his wrists out for me to see. "They are healing."

I nod and hold both of his hands between us, not even bothering to pretend I *wasn't* searching for an opportunity to check. The angry red lines from Friday are nothing more than shiny, pink marks now. "They are. How do *you* feel?"

"I'm fine."

"Really?"

He knows what I mean. Never mind all of his physical pains; how does he feel about Matthew? About heroin? About cigarettes? About us?

Dan squeezes my hands. "I feel good," he whispers. "I feel safe, and happy, and strong. I feel like I could do anything."

Okay. I need to be more direct.

"What about smoking?"

He twitches. It's a dead giveaway, and I use his moment of hesitation to push him.

"How are you doing? Have you had any today?"

He doesn't need to answer. The tightness of his jaw when he looks up and away, where I have no chance of making eye contact with him, tells me enough.

"Yes."

"How many?"

"Some." He sighs. "I am trying."

"I know." I soften my voice and squeeze his hands before he can think I'm getting impatient. "I know, Dan. Cutting down is a great start."

A frustrated little groan rumbles in his throat.

"Hey," I whisper. "You're doing brilliantly and I'm very proud—"

"It's *pathetic*," he hisses, finally looking at me again. "I should be better than this."

I purse my lips and raise an eyebrow. I wasn't with him for the first few days of his heroin recovery, but I know how ugly and painful drug withdrawal can be. Nicotine is going to be nasty too.

Dan tries to tug his hands from mine, suddenly showing real irritation. "There's no point. Today has been awful— why? Why bother?"

"*Hey*."

"William—"

"As *if* I'm gonna let go of you while you're talking like this, stupid," I mutter, twisting my wrists uncomfortably so I can lace our fingers together.

I swear to God, he nearly stomps his foot.

"You don't understand this," he says, refusing to look at me. "You never will."

"Correct." I sigh. "But that doesn't mean I'm going to let you give up. Come on, Dan. What time is it?"

I have his hands hostage, so I tilt my head and check the time on his watch. Twenty to six.

"I bet one of the pharmacies is open," I say, blinking up at him. He looks ready to cry. "We can get you some NRTs."

"Some *what*?"

Oops. "Nicotine replacement therapies. Patches or gum or something. You know, something to help with the cravings."

He looks away again. "Great. More replacements."

"You of all people can't complain about being told to take more drugs," I snap.

Dan raises an eyebrow. "Excuse me?"

I can't go back from that one. Shit. "You heard me," I grumble, holding his hands so tight the bones might shatter. "Dan, you were putting who the hell knows what into your body last year. You can't complain about being told to take something which is *safe* and *clean*—"

"It's just swapping dependency from one thing to another!"

"Yeah, from one thing which contains carcinogens to another thing which only contains the drug you're craving!"

He stares at me and I stare at him and I know this argument doesn't need to be happening. I know he's just irritated, and I'm just tired and desperate, and neither of us ever needed to raise our voices.

I let go of his hands, planning on going in for a hug, but he backs away from me. He moves with his chin held high, defensive, and doesn't stop until his back is flat against the brick wall of the stairwell.

My heart breaks.

"Daniel," I whisper. "Daniel, I'm so sorry. I know you're hurting and upset and I should be more patient with you."

He doesn't say anything. Maybe going out is a bad idea. In the strange electric light of the apartment building, his cheeks look shallow and pale. He isn't breathing.

I'm getting desperate. "I'm sorry, Dan. I shouldn't have shouted. And I shouldn't have said that."

Dan closes his eyes and drops his head, bowing his chin into his chest. It's submissive. I hate it.

"Dan—"

"I know you are trying to help," he chokes out, "but I *don't* know how to explain."

My chest aches. "Try," I whisper. "I'm listening. Try to explain."

He takes a slow breath and I inch closer.

"I don't remember it being this bad in October," he murmurs. "The prescription helped."

"Yeah." I clear my throat. "Yeah, I know it helps. Did it help right away?"

I thought it would take Dan much longer than this to give me details about this particular weekend of his life. I know about his broken ribs. I know about his therapy, but I don't know anything about those first few days without heroin.

"No," he admits. "Not for a few days."

I take his hand.

"But I hurt all over. This is—this is difficult."

The fact he's still letting me hold his hand is a good sign.

"It's like a sharp ache here," he explains, using his free hand to gesture to the side of his head, from his temple to his jaw. "And I feel dry. And restless, like there is something I forgot to do. I miss smoking."

I reach up to cover the side of his face, replacing his hand with my own. His cheek feels warm and he doesn't pull away from me, like I feared he would.

Okay. Maybe he doesn't hate me. I can't believe I said *you of all people*, though. What a dick.

"Today has been difficult."

I groan lightly. "Should you have phoned me earlier?"

Dan blinks and the mood changes. It's like he's just switched on a light. "Yes, so I could have reminded you to eat."

I grimace. "No, silly. So you could have told me that you were hurting."

He shrugs. "I should be used to it, right?"

"No, Dan—"

"Me, *of all people*."

Okay. Okay. I deserve that.

He doesn't, though.

We're not exactly in a private place, but I slide my hand so it's resting on the side of Dan's neck and stretch up on my toes. I think he thinks I'm going to kiss him, but I have something much more important to do.

"I didn't mean it like that," I tell him. "I only meant that you've spent so much time consuming *bad* drugs that I can't understand you refusing *good* ones. You know, ones that are gonna help."

Dan sighs and wraps his free arm around my back, supporting me. "Motivation is difficult."

"I know. But you're doing so well—"

"Am I?"

I sink back down onto my heels. "You are, Dan. I'm very proud of you."

His nostrils flicker. "Are you?"

Oh, Dan.

I push my arm around his shoulders and cling to him, holding us as tightly together as I can with just one arm. My other hand is still holding his, and I refuse to let go.

"Yes." I breathe deeply. "Yes. I'm so proud of you. Will you let me drag you to a pharmacy to get you some nicotine?" I pull back to watch for his reaction. "Or do you not want to do that tonight?"

Dan pouts. "As long as we are quick. You need to eat—"

"And *you* need nicotine," I counter. "Let me make you get help."

He drops his arm from around me and his pout deepens. It's incredibly cute, and if we were in his flat or in my room I'd kiss him sooner than breathe.

"Fine," he says. "But I don't apologise for being grumpy at the moment."

I grin so much it hurts. "That's fine," I say. "I can take grumpy. As long as you can take me being an idiot."

He nods. "I am used to that."

Six

Daniel does not like the cold. He especially does not like the snow.

After one more cuddle, he releases me and opens the main door, keeping hold of my hand. For half a moment, I think he's going to burst into tears.

His mouth drops open and a sad little cloud of breath curls away from him in a quiet *oh*. It's such an overreaction that I can't help but laugh.

"Come on, baby," I tease. "It's barely sticking."

Snow is falling fairly heavily from the dark, cloudy sky. The flakes glow bright where the streetlamps catch them, but I'm right—it's barely sticking. At the moment.

Dan looks heartbroken.

"I'm not a *baby*," he mutters, leaning down to kiss my cheek beneath my glasses. It feels like a special place, and it takes my breath away.

"You are when it comes to getting cold."

Sulking, he shoves his hands in his coat pockets and steps out into the snow. I'm sad to be let go of but it *is* cold.

"Safe to say you didn't grow up in a snowy part of Russia then," I say, feeling brave.

Despite our argument a few minutes ago, Dan must be feeling *good*. He doesn't brush my question away; he answers it. With more detail than I ever expected.

"No, Novosibirsk is cold," he says, voice light. *Novosibirsk*. We've never discussed exactly *where* in the great big expanse of Russia Dan's from, and I make sure to remember every word as we walk towards the pharmacy. "Maybe that is why I hate the cold so much. Reminds me of there." He gives me a sideways glance and a reassuring smirk. "You realise, though, that here is not that bad. Novosibirsk has winters at minus twenty."

"Excuse me?"

Dan nods. "This is nothing, really. Walking to school was hell."

"Fuck me."

He laughs and takes one of his hands out of his pockets to find and hold mine. "Hmm."

My cheeks burn hot enough to turn snowflakes to steam when I realise what I said.

"But that does not mean I am *comfortable* right now," Dan continues, letting us pretend nothing happened. "I hate being cold."

I smile up at him, adding all this new information to what I know about this guy I've fallen for. *Novosibirsk*. I'm gonna have to Google it.

"I know you do," I say, pulling his hand over to cuddle against my chest. "I'm surprised you aren't wearing gloves."

"I never have," he grumbles. "Not while I smoked."

I feel a pang in my chest as I think, again, about all the thousands of cigarettes he's gone through in his life. I worry about him every time he coughs, but I don't think he'd appreciate me mentioning that.

"Maybe we'll have to get you some now," I suggest, glancing up at him as we walk. Snow is settling on his blond hair, making it sparkle. I want to tell him how pretty he is, but he doesn't look happy. Worry twists through me. "And a cute hat."

Dan laughs. Thank heavens. "A hat?"

"Keep your ears warm."

He squeezes my hand and whatever was upsetting him has clearly passed, because a smile settles across his face. "Okay. Maybe that is a good idea."

"Exactly. You can't complain about being cold if you aren't even going to try to stay warm."

"I am trying," he grumbles, tugging his elbows into his sides for emphasis. I reluctantly release his hand so he can put it back in his pocket. "Here is just *miserable*. And it is always raining."

"Not true," I say. "Summer can be *hot*."

Dan grimaces, and I realise what I've done before he whispers, "I have to leave in July. And I don't come back until the very end of August. That is *if* I fail. If not…"

He can't come back until he gets a job. I know this. I know

this and I hate this.

There's another problem too. A much more selfish problem that I really should be able to brush aside. Dan leaving and getting a new VISA is vitally important, after all.

But he'll miss my birthday.

Frustrated, Dan takes his hands out of his pockets and shoves them into his hair. We keep walking in silence, neither of us wanting to be the one to mention *August*, and we've stepped through the sliding doors of the pharmacy before he sighs and takes my hand again.

"Stay near me," he whispers.

Okay. Disappointment about him not being here for my birthday—and fear for him being back in Russia—aside, I lace our fingers together and drag him to the shelf of nicotine replacement therapies. I think patches will be easiest, but Dan picks up a box of gum.

"Take both," I say, grabbing a box. He hesitates to take it from me. "It's good to use a combination. Patches for slow release, gum for a quick hit."

He narrows his eyes at me. Maybe I used the wrong phrase.

"Should we talk to someone about it?" he mutters, turning the box of patches over in his hand. "All I know so far is it hurts."

Oh, I don't like that. He's struggled so much today—so much more than he's let on. But why am I surprised? Dan's number one skill is suffering in silence.

I've got to get him all the help I can find.

I smile up at him and nod. "Let's go ask at the counter."

He hides it well, but he's trembling as we walk up to the late-shift pharmacist. Seeing us coming, she smiles and tries to make eye contact with Dan. He *is* the one clutching two distinctive green boxes.

There is every chance he'll back out of this.

"Hey," I say, taking the lead and very subtly touching my hand to the back of Dan's coat. I doubt he can feel it, but I'm ready to support him. "Can you take these together?"

I know you can.

The pharmacist peers at the boxes. "Yeah, absolutely. They for you, duck?"

Startled, Dan nods.

"He quit yesterday," I say, putting some pressure through the back of his coat. "This was the first opportunity we've had to get anything."

She nods. "That's fair enough. Yeah, you can take them together. I think—" She reaches over and takes the box of patches from Dan— "Yeah, these are ones you can wear all night. So, they're like a really slow, steady release that you change every twenty-four hours. The gum will give you more of a quick burst, like if you lit a cigarette."

Dan nods. I think that's all we're going to get out of him.

"Thanks," I say. "Do you have any other tips?"

The pharmacist rustles through some paperwork and produces a leaflet advertising a support group.

Knowing how much Dan hated his therapy group before Christmas, I can't help but think this is just a waste of a tree. We take it anyway.

"The group meets Wednesdays and Fridays," she says, "and you can just tag along. They're a lovely group, they really are. You might want to book in with your GP, especially if you find that these don't help you much."

I thank her again. We pay and Dan puts both boxes into the pockets of his coat, absolutely wordless and far too pale under the electric lights.

I let him keep his silence until we're outside, back in the swirling snow. Unfortunately for Dan, it looks like it will be snowing all night. The sky is still a heavy grey, rather than star-studded black, and snow is beginning to stick to the ground. We tread through it together, vaguely aiming towards a row of pubs. One of them will have something we'll both eat.

"You should speak to your therapist about nicotine," I say when I can't bear waiting any longer.

Dan stops walking and we make eye contact for the first time since speaking to the pharmacist. His eyes aren't so bright in the evening streetlight, but I can see the way he's frowning.

"I should," he agrees, "but I didn't. I spoke to her today, but I didn't say anything about this because I think it won't last."

Alert, alert.

I push my shoulders back and stand up straight, making sure he knows I mean business. "It's going to last forever," I say, voice clipped. "Because there is no way in hell someone who can recover from a heroin addiction *won't* recover from a nicotine addiction."

He turns his face away and I get a full view of the nasty

bruise sprawling across his eyebrow. My poor Daniel.

"Here," I say, rummaging through his pockets for the pack of gum. I pop the box and take out one sugar-coated square, balancing it between my finger and thumb. "Open up."

He side-eyes me.

"Do *not* make me force-feed you."

It works; he laughs. Instead of taking the gum from me, he puts his hands on either side of my waist and drops his mouth open so I can place the square between his teeth.

I don't think either of us is breathing. We stare at each other, unblinking and unmoving while snowflakes continue to drift around us. For a moment, I worry he'll spit the gum back out. He doesn't. He takes it very slowly into his mouth and holds my gaze while he bites, crunching it between his teeth.

He sneers as the flavour washes over his tongue, and I realise my hand is still in the air between us.

I move it to rest against the side of his neck.

"Not nice?" I ask, holding my breath while he swallows.

He just hums.

"What's it like?"

"Sadness," he mutters. I'd hoped it would be refreshing, or comforting, or at least something positive. "Sorry. We need to get you fed."

I drop my hand from his neck. "We do. We could try a patch."

Dan raises his eyebrow. "We? No. *I* will, but not now.

Not here."

"When we're back at yours then," I say, trying to not let his pedantics bother me. I know it's only *Dan* who can do this, but I want to help. Goodness, I want to help. I was useless last year while he dealt with heroin withdrawal. Why do I have to be useless now?

"Dan?" We start walking again, side by side but not holding hands. "Is there anything I can do?"

He laughs, surprised, and puts his arm across my shoulders. "Oh, William."

Will I ever get over the way he says my name? The *w* is softened, like it comes from further back in his mouth, and the *am* sounds like *um*. It makes my skin shiver in a very nice way.

"You do *everything*," he continues. "But you can start by eating lunch tomorrow, before your exam."

I groan. I don't want us thinking about me. "I just forgot."

"I know. But you do this regularly."

"You change the subject regularly."

He squeezes my shoulders. "True."

We both laugh. We probably look drunk, but I wrap my arm around Dan's waist and cuddle closer as we walk. The snow is getting heavier.

"I will try patches," he mutters. "And I'll tell Suzie tomorrow."

I take his hand where it dangles near my arm. "Suzie?"

"My therapist."

I nudge him. "Dan, you've been working with her for three months and this is the first time you've mentioned her name."

"You didn't ask."

He's got me there. I nudge him again.

"Here?" Dan asks, tugging me towards the first pub.

I don't feel like being fussy, so I nod and we walk in together.

We walk in *together*.

Dan still has his arm around me. I still have my arm around him. We're red-cheeked and glowing with love, but I'm not afraid. I'm not embarrassed. I'm not even nervous.

Okay, that's a slight lie. I feel sick and I can feel my pulse in my throat. I've never been visibly queer before, but I'm confident I'm safe. Even more importantly, I want to do this.

I walk into this building with Dan, clearly in love with him, and it's okay.

Just like that, I'm out to a whole room full of strangers.

He leads us to a small table against a wall and we have to let go of each other. It's okay, though, because now we have something else to laugh about.

I take my coat off.

We sit down facing each other and he does a double-take, looking first at his jumper and then at mine.

I laugh far too loudly.

"Ah." Dan pushes his sleeves back up to his elbows. Seeing him willingly showing off his arms is such a relief. "Is this why you were so giggly?"

"Giggly? Me?" I snigger. "Yeah, okay. It was the only nice thing I brought with me. And it's *my* colour, anyway."

He frowns and cocks his head. "What do you mean?"

I push my glasses down my nose and blink at him over the top, irises unobstructed by anti-glare. "Matches my eyes."

Dan looks like he's never been happier. "You have beautiful eyes," he says. "Please choose food."

I kick him under the table. "I will. What's your favourite colour?"

"Who is changing the subject now?"

"*Dan*."

He forces a menu into my hands. "Green. Yours?"

"Green?"

"Yes. What is yours?"

I grumble. "Orange, I think," I mutter. "Maybe bright blue—turquoise. Or like a bubble-gum pink."

Dan grins at me. "Bright, then?"

"Yeah."

"But you always wear grey."

"I do," I admit. "But that's because I don't like drawing attention to myself."

Dan's grin softens. "Yeah. I understand. Green suits you."

"See? It's my colour."

"Can we share it?"

Oh, heavens. If I wasn't already ridiculously in love with him—

"Choose dinner," he says. "Otherwise I will choose for you."

I wink at him. "Yes, we can share green," I say. "And there's no need to get bossy. I've already decided."

Dan raises an eyebrow and waits.

I haven't actually looked at the menu yet, so I guess he has a valid point. I cast my eyes down, find the *light bites* section, and relax a little when I see they still serve jacket potatoes in the evening. It was that or pizza.

"Easy," I say. "You?"

He thinks for a moment and nods. "I'll go and order. What do you want?"

I lick dry lips. "Jacket with cheese."

"Are you sure?"

I nod. "Dead sure."

"You haven't eaten all day—"

"I can always have something else when we get back to yours," I say, defensive. I've had enough of being nagged about food today, thanks.

Dan doesn't push it anymore. He stands up, touches my chin with his fingertips, and gives me a warm smile before striding to the bar to place our order.

I watch him. There isn't an ounce of nervousness about him, even as he stands between forty-year-old men who are all several pints into the evening. Dan is tall and confident and beautiful. He turns back around, catching me staring.

I burn bright red and look at my menu until he returns.

"Here," Dan says, placing a glass of water in front of me. "Have you spoken to anyone today?"

"Lilley and Cas," I admit. "They were going to the library." Not a lie. "And they wanted to know how we are." Also not a lie. But most definitely not the truth either, and I almost say,

"*I saw them when I popped into town this afternoon,*" but then I'd have to admit that I didn't eat lunch because I was too busy stressing about his Christmas presents to have an appetite. I'd ruin the surprise.

"And how *are* we?"

I look up, alarmed, but Dan's grinning at me. Maybe he likes that word as much as I do. *We. Us.*

"We're great," I say.

He sits back in his seat, eyes sparkling and cheeks lightly blushing. "We are. Tell me about revision."

I tell him about the exam papers I worked through and admit that I'm hoping he'll read the conclusion of that research paper to me. He offers to do it right now, but blushing again, I say I'd rather concentrate on it when we're alone.

Seven

There's a real risk the whole surprise might fall flat, because we have a history of falling asleep on the settee. It's just too relaxing. I'm lying close to the edge of the cushions, head resting on his arm and vaguely watching the TV. My glasses are off, though, so I can't really see what's going on. Dan is settled right behind me, legs bent to press his knees against mine, and he kisses my shoulder periodically.

I'm so in love that I could burst.

We need to go to bed, but I'm so comfortable that it takes me a few hours.

"Time for bed?" I say when the programme ends. "You can read to me when we're all cosy."

He laughs and gives me a squeeze. "We *are* cosy," he whispers. "But okay. Do you want to get up early tomorrow?"

I grumble. "Yeah. My exam isn't until one, though."

"I know," Dan whispers, shoving his face into my hair. "I don't want to risk you being late. We'll get to campus at nine, like normal. Do you want me to leave you alone?"

"Uh, *no*."

He laughs again. I would sacrifice anything to have him laugh like this every day.

"But you need to do work, don't you?"

His laughter fades to a low groan. "I do. I can work in the afternoon."

"Did you get much done today?"

Oh, his hesitation is telling.

"Enough," he says eventually, tightening his arm over my chest and pinning me in place. "Enough."

"Dan."

"I will go to the library," he concedes, 'but you have to *promise* you will eat."

I couldn't eat today, with the anticipation of this surprise Christmas. Does he really think I'll be able to eat tomorrow, with my first second-year exam looming over me?

"Stay with me for breakfast," I suggest. "That way you'll *know* I've had something—" and I'll have been *forced* to have something— "and you won't be stressing about me."

He likes that idea. He nuzzles into my hair again, hot breath warming the skin of my neck, and presses his knees more firmly into the back of mine.

"Okay," he whispers. "This is a good plan."

It is.

"Shall we go to bed?"

I know it was my suggestion, but I hesitate. I'm still doubting how good this surprise is going to be, and part of me wants to rush into his bedroom and clear it all away.

I bet he can see the nervous energy rolling from me. I'm excited about this, yeah, but still terrified that I've completely got the wrong angle. This might break his heart. This might be a very bad end to the day.

I don't move. "Dan?"

"Hmm?"

I hesitate. Is this the worst idea ever? "Say something in Russian."

I haven't asked him to for weeks—not since that first time. He hums, tightens his arm around my chest, and kisses my hair. It makes my eyelids flutter.

"Тебе нужно лечь спать."

What a relief. I snuggle backwards into him and lift his hand so I can kiss his palm. "And that would be?"

"You need to go to bed," he translates. "Я так тебя люблю."

I close my eyes, somewhat reassured. I'm probably eighty percent confident that he's going to like the surprise. "I love you too, Dan. How do you feel about it all now?"

"It?"

Oops. "Home."

"*You* are home," he whispers. "*You* have been home for months."

I make him fold his fingers so I can kiss his knuckles. "Okay. How do you feel about Russia?"

I know it's ridiculous, but saying *Russia* around him terrifies me. For a start, the word sounds so coarse and heavy in my accent. Dan just can't help but roll the *R*.

"Unhappy," he admits. "I have to go back. I don't like the thought of leaving you."

I don't like it either. I kiss his knuckles again. "Yeah. I don't want you to go, but I guess we don't have a choice."

"Not really, darling."

Darling.

I can't get caught up thinking about how lovely it is to be called *darling*. Now is not the time.

"But you seem happier with the language," I press. "You're not so...embarrassed."

He makes a disbelieving sound in the back of his throat. "Are you sure? I could not speak to the pharmacist."

"I thought that was a drug thing."

He laughs. "No, that was an accent thing."

I blink at the room. "Oh."

Seventy percent.

"Sometimes I'm reminded how much of a stereotype I am," he whispers. "A traumatised heroin addict who has smoked since fifteen."

"Correction," I say, giving his hand a squeeze. "A *recovered* heroin addict who has also *quit* smoking *and* who is gay. And who hates the cold."

"I think we all hate the cold."

"We?"

"Russians."

Oh, my God.

It's a small thing. It's an impossibly small *linguistic* thing, and maybe I'm thinking too deeply about this. But Dan just claimed his nationality. He just counted himself as one of the group, rather than as the outsider he's always considered himself to be.

Eighty percent.

I could kill Matthew for ever making Dan doubt himself.

"Well," I breathe, "tell the rest of the world that. Everyone thinks you walk around in shorts until it reaches minus twenty."

Dan shudders at the thought. "No, thank you."

I chuckle again and twist onto my back so I can see him. He keeps his arm around me but leans into the cushions, giving me space to move.

"This is what I mean," I say, dropping his hand so I can touch his face instead. "You seem less upset by it all. Before New Zealand, you could barely talk about Russia."

Dan shrugs one shoulder and slides his hand down to rest over the front of my waist. Lying on my back, there's a gap between my body and the waistband of my jeans. I need to get a belt.

"It is easier now I know you do not mind."

Eighty-five percent. Maybe pushing ninety.

I roll my eyes. "Don't mind? I've told you before. It's just part of you, Dan. It's like saying *I don't mind* you have blue eyes."

He smirks and blushes, cheek warming up under my hand. As if we're not already warm enough. It's very intimate cuddled together like this on his settee.

"Actually, that *is* a stereotype you fill," I warn him. "Tall, blond, blue eyes—"

"Spanish mother," he counters. Oh, my goodness. Are we going to talk about all of his ghosts tonight? I'm more than happy to. It's like a layer of smoke lifts from around him with each one, bringing him more and more into focus. He already dazzles me.

I draw a line with my fingertip up from the corner of his mouth to his hairline near his eye. "Yeah," I say. "Got those Eastern European cheekbones, though."

He blushes again and it's so beautiful, and so perfectly pure, that I push myself up on my elbow to kiss him before he can see the tears that just filled my eyes.

It's not a big kiss. It's not a long kiss, or one that would ever lead to anything more than a pair of smiles, but I love it.

"I love you," I say, noting the way my heart skips. It does it every time I say it, and I'm not sure that's ever going to change. "We should go to bed."

I'm confident now that he isn't going to hate the little nod to his nationality. Actually, I think he'll love it.

Eight

It's another few minutes before we so much as open the bedroom door. First, Dan makes us make drinks and tries to convince me to eat something else, but I point out we need to brush our teeth.

I duck into the bedroom to drop off my glasses and grab my wash bag without him seeing the little tree on his bedside table.

"You seem tired," Dan whispers, looking at me through the corner of his eye while we share the washbasin. "And you haven't started exams yet."

I grunt. "It's gonna be hell."

"You should have eaten more tonight." He sighs. "You will struggle, won't you?"

I pull a face. "Yeah," I admit around my toothbrush, "but I'll be all right. I'll have breakfast, then we'll meet up again for tea. Yeah?"

He smirks at me in the mirror. "Tea? You do not mean

the drink."

I nudge him with my elbow and finish scrubbing my teeth. "You know exactly what I mean."

"Ужин," he says. "Instead of обед."

Is he...trying to teach me?

I nod once, doing my very best to commit those words to memory. "Обед. What's that?"

"Lunch."

I nod and lean down to wash my toothbrush. "So, that was *dinner* and *lunch*?"

His smirk cracks into a huge grin and damn, I love him.

Have I ever seen him this happy? Probably not. He's glowing with pride, freshly brushed teeth sparkling in the electric bathroom light, and seems a million miles away from the nervous guy I took home to my bedroom that first night.

I keep those two words running through my head while I wash my face, hoping this is something we'll do regularly now. Maybe he'll teach me a new word each night. Maybe we'll get to the point where we can have conversations in his first language.

Maybe I should take it upon myself to learn.

It could be a nice break from medicine revision.

Dan realises we haven't turned the TV off and leaves me alone in the bathroom for a moment. I'm not sure when we started sharing the bathroom, but it's nice. We haven't quite gone as far as using the toilet with each other in the room, but I've considered waiting on the other side of the shower door with him while he washes. Especially this last weekend.

I try to push away the memories of Dan's bleeding eyebrow and trembling hands, but they creep in, lurking in the shadows in the corners of my vision.

I blink. They're still there, and I remember Dan's terrified whimpering and crying from Friday night as if it's happening right now. I can hear him moving around the living room, tidying our shoes away and making sure things are turned off. He isn't upset.

And yet—

"Daniel?"

"Yes?"

I hesitate. I'm being silly.

"William?"

"How are you?"

He laughs, appearing in the doorway like a beam of sunlight. Just seeing him clearly feeling all right pushes those memories away, and I start to blush. Of course he's okay. He just taught me two words in Russian while we brushed our teeth—Dan couldn't be more okay if he tried.

He doesn't act like I'm overreacting, though. He leans against the doorframe and smiles, watching me while I dry my hands. "I am fine, darling. How are you?"

A fair question. I shrug and put my toothbrush on the side, ready for morning. "All right. Tired, yeah."

Dan waits in the doorway, knowing I haven't been completely honest.

"I'm worried about you," I admit.

"I know."

"I know I shouldn't worry, because it doesn't help, but—"

"It is what you do best," he whispers.

I look up and make eye contact with him.

"You are allowed to worry, but there is no need."

I raise an eyebrow. "Worried about your nightmares, your eyebrow, you relapsing, you leaving—"

He rolls his eyes and steps to stand behind me, close enough so that the front of his body is pressed softly against the back of mine. I hold my breath. "My nightmares are nothing new. This," he turns his face to bump his bruised eyebrow against my hair, "does not hurt now. I will try the patches and I'm not leaving, William, unless you ask me to."

"Not gonna happen."

He chuckles and kisses my hair. "I hope not. I've just got used to being with you every day."

I grin and decide it's time to stop blocking him from his bedroom. I dry my hands and face, lean back into his arms for a quick cuddle, and flick the light off. "Bedtime," I say.

Dan lets go of me and leads the way out of the bathroom, across the corner of his living room, and to his bedroom door.

My nervous heart thunders. I wish I'd done more. I wish I'd known sooner. I wish I'd got him an actual present.

Dan pushes open the door and steps inside.

I left the light on when I grabbed my wash bag, so everything is in full view. The tinsel across the headboard looks dull and lacklustre. The tree is barely decorated and squashed at a funny angle.

Dan stops still, hand falling heavily from the door.

Good reaction? Bad reaction?

I chew the inside of my cheek. If he gets upset, I'll say it's because we missed having Christmas together. I won't mention Russia.

"William," he whispers, voice thick and heavy.

I inch closer and put my hand on his waist from behind. I can't bring myself to step into the bedroom—I can't bring myself to look at his face.

"Спасибо."

A tickle of excitement runs through me. "Спасибо?" I echo, blushing even though I'm sure I pronounced it okay.

"Thank you," he translates. "You—you did not need to."

"Is it okay, though? We can just pretend it's left over from December Christmas if you don't like it."

Subtle, Will.

Dan turns and tugs me into his chest without giving me a chance to see his face. He holds me with more force than usual, crushing my shoulders and making it impossible for me to step back even if I wanted to.

"I didn't expect you to know," he whispers.

I have to be honest. "Lilley told me," I admit, voice muffled by his jumper. "Ran around town this afternoon like a mad thing trying to find anything even remotely Christmassy."

Dan chuckles. "How did she know?"

"Cassie was doing some research."

He hums a happy little sound and rubs his hand down my back. "How are they both?"

"Good, I think." Why are we changing the subject? Is

he embarrassed? Annoyed? "They've loved each other for a while."

"I can see that." He kisses my hair. "I should have cooked for you."

Okay, we're back to the present. "Nah, you bought me dinner. That was more than enough." An exciting thought hits me. "Was that our first date?"

"I think it was," he murmurs. "I liked it."

Smiling is beginning to hurt. "So did I."

"Did I see coffee by the tree?"

I snort a laugh and wriggle free of his arms so I can finally get a look at his face. His eyelids are red and there's a pinkness to his nose that I haven't seen many times. I won't embarrass him by pointing it out. Instead, I reach up to push his hair back from his forehead and kiss his jaw.

He grunts and leans down so I can kiss him properly.

We're both minty and it is *very* nice. I'll ignore the fact he was just crying if he ignores that I'm having to cling to his arms to reach. When I open my eyes and steal a glance at him, his eyelids are shut and they twitch every so often, like he thought about opening them.

I would kiss him forever.

Everything about Dan is warm. His hands on my waist are warm through my jumper. His breath is warm where it flutters across my face. His dry lips are warm against mine and when I tease them open, I find that his tongue is warm too.

His hands find my cheeks and push me away, holding me so there's just an inch between us.

My legs are beginning to shake.

"Bedtime," he whispers.

I nod. "You need to open your card."

"What?" Dan looks past me to the sad Christmas offerings. "A card?"

I laugh and return to my normal height. I can't move away from him, though. It's like that kiss turned on some gravity between us and it's useless to fight against it. "Yep. Christmas card, because it's Christmas."

Dan casts warm, soft eyes down at me and *I* nearly cry.

"It's Christmas," he echoes.

We're in real danger of staring at each other for the rest of the night, so I tear myself from his arms and walk over to my side of the bed.

"Come on," I say. "Let's get settled and then you can open your card and read this conclusion to me. Maybe you can tell me about Christmas too."

Dan's laugh is like a hug. "What would you like to know?"

"Everything," I say, getting into bed. It's still a thrill to lie beside him, even though we've done this for months now. "But once you're comfy."

Dan sighs very quietly and I only just now remember that he needs to try one of those nicotine patches. He takes the box out of his back pocket where he must have stashed it a few minutes ago, sits on the edge of the bed, and lets me take the instructions leaflet from him.

I skim-read.

"You can place it anywhere, but arms or chest is best," I

summarise. "We'll have to change it at this time tomorrow."

"Okay." He doesn't move.

I understand and open one of the patches. I can't give him space to hesitate, because we both know how easy it would be for Dan to run outside and light a cigarette, so I have to take the lead. This is something he *will* let me help with.

"Where do you want it?"

Dan sighs again and tugs his jumper over his head. The soft white t-shirt he has on underneath must be warm, because it's so close to his skin, but I don't reach out and touch it, as much as I'd like to. I don't want to distract him.

"Here?" he suggests, tapping the top of his left arm with his right hand.

I think that's a very good idea, so I waste no time in peeling the back off the patch and smoothing it on to his skin.

"Thank you," he mutters. He takes his jeans off but keeps his t-shirt on, so we're a little bit like opposites when I shimmy into my pyjama trousers.

"Thought you'd warmed up," I comment, smiling at him as he tugs the duvet up to his chin.

He makes a tight noise in the back of his throat and shows me his phone screen. He has it open to a web browser and tonight's forecast, which has a little snowflake and a few light clouds. "It is *minus three*," he hisses.

"Yes, but that's *outside*."

"I know."

I just laugh at his stubbornness and settle back against the headboard, trying to not be self-conscious that I'm bare-chested and he isn't. It doesn't matter. It really doesn't matter. "You can open your card now," I say. "Don't get too excited."

I thought he'd laugh. Instead, Dan's perfectly quiet as he takes the card from his bedside table. He stares at the front for much longer than I think is needed. It's just a drawing of a Christmas wreath, embossed with gold and underwritten with *Merry Christmas*.

I hold my breath, ridiculously nervous, as he opens the card and reads my scrawled message.

To Daniel,
I hope to spend every Christmas with you. Thank you for being you.
All of my love,
William X

Dan closes the card and stands it up beside the little tree. I wish I could have found some fairy lights.

We haven't turned the light off, and he still needs to take his prescription. We must remember at the same time, because he hops out of bed and hits the switch without a word.

He settles back beside me, still silent, and covers his face. *Oh.*

"Hey," I whisper, reaching nervously for him. "Hey, Dan—"

His breathing hitches.

"Shit," I mutter. "Dan, I'm sorry—"

He drops his hands and grabs me, pulling me over into his chest. I land heavily and let out a little *huff*, cheek smushed against his shoulder. I'm glad I left my glasses off.

Dan trembles with barely contained sobs and honestly, it's a little bit scary.

I hold onto him and he holds onto me and he just…cries.

He cries for quite a few minutes.

I twist, getting comfy, and let him ride it out. He's holding me so tightly it pinches my skin, and he doesn't move his hands for all the time it takes for his breathing to come back to normal.

I don't really want to ask what happened.

I don't know what to say.

"Uhm." He sniffs, slowly releasing me.

I push my arms around his back and cling on. "Sorry."

"Don't apologise." He takes a long, deep breath that stretches his chest and lifts me. He keeps me waiting for an explanation for so long that, by the time he whispers again, my arms ache. "I wonder how you could love me." He breathes deeply. "I wonder how you, who could have the world, could love *me*."

"How? Like breathing."

"I can't understand."

"Why?"

He groans. "I'm not used to it. Thank you, darling."

I tut and get more comfortable, still lying across him but with my left arm supporting me against the mattress so we can look at each other. I'll fall asleep on top of him if he needs it.

"You're nice," I whisper. "You're nice to be around and you make me feel like everything's okay. What's not to love?"

He purses his lips. "Addict, trauma."

"You don't need me to explain to you why neither of those are reasons to not love someone, do you?"

He fidgets. "Sex."

"What about it, hon?"

His bright eyes find me through the dim room. "I don't want it."

I reach up to cup his cheek. "So?"

"*So,* what is the point?"

I don't like that. "The point, Dan, is that being around you makes me feel warm and happy. Not being around you does the opposite. Being allowed to tell you I love you makes that warm feeling even stronger—and that's all I need."

He closes his eyes. Maybe I've been too pushy and dramatic and romantic.

"I wish I could give you the world," he whispers. "I wish I could be everything perfect."

I rub my thumb across the skin beneath his eye. "Just give me you," I say. "You and time."

His eyes open again.

"This is going to take us both a while to get used to, isn't it?" I point out. "Don't doubt us before we've started."

"I am not doubting us." He starts to slide down the headboard, sinking into the pillows. "I am just overwhelmed that you would give me so much of you."

I let go of him so we can both get more comfortable. Dan finally lies down and I cuddle into his side, tucked under his arm with my head on his shoulder. It's warm. It's safe. I think Dan stops doubting me for a few minutes.

"I'll give you everything of me," I murmur, voice muffled by his shoulder. "Everything. I know we've only technically been dating since Friday, but you know I've loved you for longer than that."

Dan relaxes. "You love me."

It's not a question. He's just now understanding what I've been telling him for days, and I think this is why he cried at the card.

He didn't believe me until now.

I cuddle him tighter.

Despite Dan complaining that it's cold, the heating is on and cuddling him is a lot like holding a hot water bottle. Tucked up in his bed, in the safety of his room, is the perfect place to be during January.

I have to admit to him that I can't stand Christmas pudding, but he takes it very well.

"That's fine," he says brightly, turning the box over in his hands before putting it back under the tree on the bedside table. "What is this?"

In the dim light, I can just about make out the shining silver foil of the chocolate coins. I grin.

"What, you've never seen them before?"

Dan shakes his head.

"Open the bag."

Wordless, Dan pushes his fingers through the plastic net and tugs. He takes one of the coins out and, through the darkness, I see him raise an eyebrow. "Is this chocolate?"

I laugh, taking the coin from him and peeling both sides of the foil away. "Trust me?"

He laughs with me and drops his lips open again, like earlier. Electricity sparkles through the pit of my stomach as I reach up and attempt to put the coin into his mouth.

Dan only lets me feed him half of it before biting a piece off and moving away, stretching so he's out of reach.

For a moment, I'm stunned.

"Interesting," he says, chewing and swallowing quickly. "I do not know when I last had chocolate."

I stare at him. "What?"

"Haven't you noticed?"

He's loving this. The electricity in me has morphed into nervous butterflies and I hold my breath, waiting while he slowly decides to explain himself.

"I avoid dairy," he whispers, voice gentle. He doesn't want me to feel bad about this, but I do. "You really did not notice?"

Well...damn.

"I—no," I admit. "Any reason?"

Even in the darkness, I see the way he grimaces. His bright teeth reflect what little light is making its way into his room from the streetlight outside. "I do not tolerate it."

"*What*?"

He laughs and takes the half-eaten coin from my faltering

hand.

"You have a dairy intolerance?"

"Yes?" It sounds like a question.

"Is it milk or lactose?" I ask, as if the difference really matters.

Dan shrugs. "Lactose."

"I made you eat pizza *so* many times!"

"Please do not worry," he says, laughing. Has he met me? "I feel confident enough with you now to tell you. Can we ignore the last few months?"

"You want me to ignore the fact you regularly let me feed you food that hurts you?"

"Yes."

He says it so bluntly, and so plainly, that I don't dream of arguing with him. This is just another layer of protection for Dan. Who am I to demand he tells me things? Who am I to complain that he didn't tell me sooner?

I make sure he can see my smile and inch closer to him, bumping our arms together. "Lucky for both of us that I *love* chocolate."

"Do you really?"

"Yes."

He smirks through the darkness. The hand holding the half-eaten chocolate coin rises between us, knuckles grazing delicately across the underside of my jaw. I think I'd planned on shaving today, but that clearly went out the window. Dan's hand makes a soft scratching noise against my stubble and my breathing stops.

"Trust me," he whispers.

I've already brushed my teeth.

Regardless, I open my mouth and let him feed me the slightly melted coin. It's overwhelmingly sweet and, now that I'm thinking about dairy, I can really taste the milk. I think about every time Dan ate pizza with me, just because it was the easiest food I could think of, and I wonder how many of his sleepless nights were a joint effort between nightmares and stomach cramps.

He rests his fingertips against my cheek while I chew and swallow.

My throat is tight. I swallow again, trying to get the taste of chocolate out of my mouth, and smile at him.

"I do not think I'm missing much," he whispers.

I swallow again. "Maybe not."

"Shall I put them away?"

My heart flutters. I mean to say *yes*, but all I can manage is a nod, and Dan unceremoniously drops the net of chocolate coins onto the floor down his side of the bed.

And then he catches my face between both of his hands and holds me still for a short, sweet kiss. He lingers with the tip of his nose touched against mine and we breathe quietly, sharing this moment of closeness.

"I'm gonna buy you some lip salve," I murmur, eyes closed.

"What?"

"Your lips are so dry."

Dan chuckles, breath hitting against my face, and rubs his

thumbs into my zygomatics. "I blame the cold."

Not sure how to reply to that, I kiss him. Like each one before, it's a gentle and loving kiss. It's a kiss which says *I'm glad to be here* rather than *I want you*, and I think that's important.

Dan is ridiculously attractive. He's tall, he's beautiful, he's smart. His cocky little smirk and his ocean eyes know it too. He's gentle. He's warm.

I love him with every single part of me and, if Dan isn't interested in sex—now or ever—that's fine. It doesn't make a difference.

I just want to be able to see him when I wake up in the morning. I want to be able to hold his hand, and laugh at him pulling faces at the snow, and wake up with him at three in the morning when he has nightmares.

Our lips break apart and my eyelids flutter open.

Dan stares at me, waiting, and I smile.

"I love you," I whisper. "Can't believe you didn't tell me about lactose, though."

Dan brushes my hair back and hits me with that smirk. "Give me time and I will tell you more."

My eyes grow. "More?"

He shrugs and I don't want to push him, but damn. My boyfriend is just full of secrets.

Boyfriend.

"I will tell you soon," he promises. "But we need to sleep. We can talk more about me tomorrow."

Okay, he's embarrassed. The last thing I want to do is push

him for more details and make him uncomfortable, so I nod and try to pull free of his hands.

He lets me, but only after dropping a very gentle kiss onto the arch of my cheek. "I love you too," he says quickly, like he doesn't want me to think he forgot I said it. "Thank you for Christmas."

I grin so much it hurts my cheeks. "You're welcome," I whisper, settling down onto my pillow and watching him as he copies me. "Prescription, Dan."

He groans and twists onto his right side to take the tablet from its box on his bedside table.

"I'm not sure I believe you remembered it every day in New Zealand," I say while he crinkles plastic and puts the box away. "Did you?"

Dan rolls to face me again. He'll lie on his front soon and fall asleep like he does every night. "Did I what?"

"Did you take your prescription every day while you were away?"

He nods firmly. "I set a reminder."

"Very smart." I take a long, slow breath and try to calm myself down for sleep. The whole room smells like *Dan,* and I close my eyes. "Have you ever missed a dose?"

"A few times," he admits.

"What happened?" Why did I ask that? Why did I choose the moment we're about to fall asleep to ask about his addiction recovery? What the hell is wrong with me?

Dan's right hand twists through my hair, smoothing the curls back and away from my face. "If I leave it for hours, I get a headache. When I missed whole days, I was sick."

"Sick?"

"You know."

"Right." He means physically sick. I'm already lying pretty close to him, but I shuffle closer and let my arm rest over his back. "Maybe you should set that alarm again."

"I will," he says, keeping his hand in my hair, "so you do not worry about me through your exam."

"Nah, I won't worry about you," I whisper. "I know you're able to look after yourself. I just like to know I can help, y'know?"

"I know. I like to know I can help you too."

That's a nice thought. For a moment, I remember how impossible I found it to eat lunch with Lil and Cas—and I wonder if that's something I should try explaining to him. But what's to explain? I'm stressed. Eating food just gets in the way when I'm stressed like this.

Plus, I've already promised to let him make me eat breakfast in the morning. Part of me thinks he probably understands my relationship with food better than I do, and I'm struck by the realisation that he does, honestly, look after me as much as I look after him.

"You do help me," I whisper. "I think we should go to sleep now, though."

Dan hums. "You are already nearly there." He takes his hand from my hair slowly, like he hates to leave, and turns onto his front. I keep my hand on his back, drawn to his warmth and using the steady rhythm of his breathing to help myself relax.

"Night, Dan."

"С Рождеством, William."

Nine

Dan jolts awake at some dark hour where the world is almost silent and the streetlamp light is beginning to look ghostly through his curtains.

He sits up and throws the duvet away from himself, almost backhanding me in the process. I blink rapidly and whisper his name, trying to calm him down, but I'm used to this.

"Moment," he says, so heavily accented that I'm not sure if he's speaking English or Russian. But then he swears, and it's definitely in English.

"I'm right here," I whisper, watching helplessly as he leaps to his feet and paces a few lengths of the bedroom. "Keep breathing, Dan. Do you want me to make drinks?"

He shakes his head but opens the door and strides out into the rest of his flat. I expect he's going to make himself a drink, but the bathroom light switches on.

I sit up. "Dan?"

The sudden sound of him throwing up makes me shiver, but I leap from bed, launching myself at the door in time to hear him whimper my name.

"I'm here," I say, crouching behind him and putting my hands on each shoulder. "What is it? Is it withdrawal?"

I'll be concerned if it is. I sat there while he took his prescription. Has he built up a tolerance for it? He still has regular appointments with the doctor on campus, but does he need one sooner? Like, tomorrow morning?

He shakes his head and takes a sudden, tight, rasping breath. "Dreams."

I slide my hands down and around his chest. "They aren't usually this bad."

He shakes his head again and leans forward. I know what to expect and reach for some toilet paper while he throws up again, so I'm ready to wipe his face as soon as it stops.

"You don't need to," he mumbles, draped across the toilet like a limp vine.

I ignore him.

I get rid of the tissue, flush, and stretch up to dampen a new wad of tissue under the tap.

Dan gasps when I touch the cold to his cheek, but his shoulders relax. His eyelids flicker.

"Wanna tell me about it?" I ask, dabbing delicately at his face.

He shrugs.

"I think it will help."

"Probably," he admits. Another nasty breath shakes his

chest and I press closer, wishing he didn't go through this so often.

He always has nightmares. This has been a constant throughout our friendship, and I certainly didn't expect this to change just because we're dating.

"It is easier and harder each day," he whispers. "I think I am okay. But then I remember something, and I can't breathe."

I kiss his shoulder. "He's not here."

"I know." He gasps again. "But I forget when we sleep."

I hate this. I wish I could take all of his pain away, but he's been hurting like this for so long that I wouldn't even know where to begin with making him feel better. All I can do is be here for him.

"I am sorry for being sick," he murmurs, and the sound of my heart breaking is audible even over his terrible breathing.

"Take that back," I whisper. "You know it wasn't something you had any control over."

He groans.

"Daniel."

He laughs nervously and leans into me, right into my chest.

I soften my voice. "I love you."

He hums and takes the damp tissue from me. "I love you. Thank you."

"Wanna tell me more?"

"Can I brush my teeth?"

Fine. I give him a gentle squeeze and let him get up, standing back while he flushes the toilet and washes. His breathing is still bad.

"Better?" I ask, timidly putting my hands on his shoulders.

He nods.

"Want a drink? Or back to bed?"

"Bed," he whispers. "You need to sleep."

"But do you need a drink?"

"No," he says firmly. "Let's go to bed."

Fine. I kiss his shoulder again and lead him out of the bathroom to his bedroom.

Our bedroom?

Dan turns lights off as we go so when we're back in bed, we're in darkness. He groans softly and I hear the rattle of his box of nicotine gum before he sits back against the headboard, chewing.

I sit right beside him.

"I may be ill tomorrow," he says lowly. "I do not know how well my prescription will work."

I take his hand. "It's nothing you can't handle."

"Thank you."

I let him pause while he chews, building up to sharing whatever else it is that's upset him. In the quiet, it would be easy to fall back to sleep.

"He is out of the hospital."

The darkness seeps from the room and into my chest. "Okay," I say, sounding like I'm on the other side of the door. "Tell me everything."

He takes a long, slow breath. It's an improvement on the gasping and holding of the last few minutes, but I'm tense enough to snap.

"Today."

"Okay." I take his hand. "Have you spoken to him?"

"No."

Too quick.

I rest my head on his shoulder and wait.

"Yes."

I bite the inside of my cheek, giving us both time to react. I hate this. I hate this.

Dan sighs and picks his phone up from where it's lying on charge. He taps in his pin and hands it to me, giving me the power to navigate to his texts and find the very short conversation with an unsaved number.

All of the messages are from today.

11:02 I'm out and getting help. Sorry for everything I put you through. See you soon? Matthew x

12:30 How are you? X

14:44 Dan? How are you? X

14:57 Daniel: I'm glad you are okay. Don't text me again

**15:02 Are you okay
though? I miss you x**

**15:38 Did you have a nice
new year? I never asked x**

16:05 Is he okay? X

**17:13 What are you
doing this evening? x**

"He keeps texting," Dan says, even though I can see it for myself. "I don't know."

"We were meant to get you a new number," I mutter through gritted teeth. "You could have gone today."

He shakes his head. "Didn't trust myself."

"Okay." Of all the reasons he could have given, that's the best one. The most responsible one. The most terrifying one. I snuggle closer, protective, and do my best to not think of all the reasons he couldn't trust himself. "First thing tomorrow, we'll go into town and get you a new SIM card. Then we can get the bus to campus and have breakfast in the SU, maybe."

He kisses my hair. "We can taxi."

"Missing the most important point, babe."

"Thank you."

I reach over him to put his phone back onto the bedside table but I don't go back to my pillow. I stay draped across him, cheek against his chest, and we both breathe quietly for a moment. I feel like I'm shielding him.

"I'm proud of you," I say. "I'm so proud of you for keeping yourself safe today."

He wraps his arms around me.

"And for not replying to him."

"But I did."

"Just that once, Dan. To tell him to go away."

His arms tighten. "Yeah."

"That's a really *good* thing."

He thinks about that for a minute. I'm not especially comfortable curled up like this, but I could fall asleep here. Dan is warm and listening to his steady heartbeat is like a lullaby.

"We could be on campus by ten," Dan says, "but is that early enough?"

"Yes."

"I do not want you to be stressed."

"I'll be *way* less stressed if I know he can't contact you anymore," I point out. "I think we both will."

He slides down a couple of inches towards his pillow, moving me with him. "I agree. Thank you. I know you are bored of this."

Confused, I push myself up on my arms so we can make eye contact. "Bored? Excuse me?"

"Of me and Matthew."

I roll my eyes. "*Bored* isn't the right word. Frustrated for you, yeah. Scared. Worried. But I'm not *bored*—it's not like it's a *boring* thing. It's damn terrifying."

He nods, letting me know he understands, and puts one of his hands on my waist.

"I hate him *so much*," I whisper. "I don't think you will ever understand just how much I *hate* him."

"I hate him too," Dan says. "But..."

I wait.

"But I loved him. It is difficult."

I kiss his cheek. "I know. But you're doing really brilliantly. I'm proud of you—and I mean it."

He smirks. "Proud?"

"Fucking *proud* and don't try to fight me on this one."

Instead of arguing, he kisses me. I get a taste of his gum and it's *strange*—especially second-hand. Not like that stops me from kissing him back, though.

I break away and rest my chin on his shoulder. We just hold each other, like physical contact is going to solve everything, and I think some of the stress leaves the room. I don't feel as dark or as heavy as I did a few moments ago.

"You need to sleep," he whispers. "I'm sorry for waking you."

"Don't you worry about it," I say, like I say every night. I sit up again and put myself safely back on my side of the bed. "I'm always right here when you need me."

"I know." Dan breathes slowly, getting comfortable. First, he spits out his gum and wraps it in a piece of tissue to deal with in the morning. He lies on his left side and faces me, smiling gently. His right hand rests between us and I lean forward to kiss it.

He laughs.

Every time Dan laughs, a little piece of the fear surrounding me lifts. I care less about what my family is going to say when I come out to them. I care less about how much it will hurt when he inevitably has to leave the country to update his VISA. When he's happy, I can brush away some of the aches of the last week and it all starts to feel like a terrible but distant nightmare.

"I love you," he says, like it's as easy as breathing.

It *is* as easy as breathing.

I kiss his hand again, grinning, and close my eyes.

"I love you too." Always have. Always will. "Wake me if it happens again."

He sighs. "Okay. I promise."

I grab hold of his hand and cuddle it to my chest. I imagine he'll roll onto his front soon, but it will be nice to at least fall asleep holding hands.

"Goodnight again, Dan."

Ten

Dan's alarm goes off. I guess I've been sleeping fairly lightly, because my eyes snap open and I'm wide awake.

Early dawn light is pushing around the edge of the curtains and highlighting Dan's sleeping face in a cool orange. For a moment I just gaze at him, stomach in a familiarly tight knot, but his alarm is still going.

"Dan," I whisper. "Daniel?"

Nothing. He's sleeping peacefully and it feels like a sin to wake him—especially after how upset he was last night.

"Hon, your alarm's ringing." I glide my thumb across his cheekbone and he shivers. "Hey there. Morning."

Dan squints at me, groggy and tired, and kisses the inside of my wrist. I never get to see him like this—he's always awake before me—so I savour it. His eyes close again and, for a moment, I think he's going back to sleep.

"Доброе утро," he whispers. "Are you okay?"

He's barely conscious. This is golden. If it weren't for the annoying buzzing of his alarm, I'd let us stay like this for another hour or so.

"I'm okay." I chuckle. "Your alarm is going off, Dan."

He blinks at me and lifts his head an inch from the pillow. His cheeks pinch pink and he sits up, twisting sharply to turn off the alarm.

My chuckle dies in my throat. He clearly just didn't hear it, and I wonder how many of those times I thought he was ignoring me were him actually just...not hearing.

I'm not going to say anything. This feels like another one of Dan's *I'll tell you soon* secrets.

"You're so cute when you sleep," I say instead, catching his hand before he can get out of bed. "Wait a minute."

Dan looks at me. He's trying to not look embarrassed, but his cheeks are still brighter than usual.

"I just..." I shuffle closer to him. "I love you, Dan."

He loops his arm around me and tugs me into his chest. Perfect. He's lovely and warm from sleeping, and there's something beautiful about the way he smells this early in the day.

"I love you too," he murmurs. "Are you okay? You were awake."

I shrug and close my eyes, making the most of this moment. I'm doing a good job of *not* thinking about the fact I have an exam this afternoon. "Yeah. I just woke up with your alarm—don't worry."

He kisses my hair. My eyelids flutter and I hold my breath as a shiver of electricity runs through me, down my spine from my head right to my feet.

I think Dan feels it too. Maybe it's tension from last night, or the leftover warmth from when we shared that chocolate coin, but the way we're clinging to each other feels heavy with something. Physically putting space between us is going to be a challenge.

He doesn't push me away so he can get coffee, like I thought he would. Instead, he turns towards me and holds me closer.

This is... This is heaven. This is perfect. Every morning could be like this and I would never have any complaints. Dan's warmth surrounds me like a heavy blanket and I'm safe and calm, no matter what anxiety my brain tries to dredge up. So what, I have an exam in a few hours? So what, Matthew texted him again? So what, I'm starting placements in a couple of weeks? Nothing can touch me—nothing can hurt me—while Dan and I are so peaceful.

But damn it. We do need to get up. We need to get dressed and get ourselves to a phone shop so he can buy a new SIM. We need to go to campus, we need to eat breakfast like I promised, and I need to make sure—again—that I have everything ready for my exam.

I sigh.

"Are you nervous?" he asks.

"About what?"

"Your exam.'

"Oh, God. Yeah."

Dan groans and kisses my hair again. "If we get up, you

can tell me about some of it before the shop."

I squish him as tight as I can. It presses the air from his lungs and he laughs, breathless, as I try and fail to hide from the day.

"William."

"You're so *warm*." I groan, letting go of him and admitting that our gentle moment in bed is over. "Promise me something."

"Anything."

I laugh. "Careful," I mutter, grabbing my glasses. "You don't know what I'm asking yet."

Dan just smirks at me, waiting.

"We'll *cook* dinner tonight."

He laughs and gets out of bed, pausing to smile before leaving the room. "Promise."

The sound of him walking around his kitchen and running water is blissfully domestic. I lie across the bed, head on Dan's pillow, and smile quietly to myself.

Yes, I have an exam this afternoon. But I've prepared for it. I run through some citations in my head, visualise some of the diagrams with my handwriting scribbled across them, and practice some slow breaths. The most important thing in an exam is to stay calm. I *know* everything.

Dan creeps back into the bedroom before the kettle boils and I squint at him.

"I want to try this," he says, grabbing the bag of so-called Christmas coffee. "Would you like some?"

I shake my head. "All for you, hon."

He *winks* at me. "Thought so. Water?"

"Please."

Dan saunters back out to the kitchen, standing tall with his shoulders back and the coffee bag swinging from his left hand. He's happy. He's confident.

I fucking love him.

A few minutes later, he comes back with a glass of water for me and a mug of steamy, dark filter coffee for him.

Wait a second.

"Dan, you always have milk in your fridge."

He settles down on the edge of the bed and nods.

"Why? If you don't drink it, why do you have it?"

We make eye contact, and I can't believe I even had to ask. The longer we look at each other, the more his cheeks blush. It's adorable.

"God, you're cute," I mumble, sitting up and pushing my arms around him. He laughs, nervous, and hands me my glass. "You've been getting it for me, haven't you?"

"Yes."

"You're so..." I want to say stupid, but that's entirely the wrong word. "Thoughtful. Damn it, Dan. Maybe I should start having cereal before we leave or something."

It's like I just turned a light on. Dan positively beams at me, blue eyes sparkling with more than just caffeine, and he seems to be holding his breath.

"Do you mean that?"

My stomach twists a little, but I nod.

"There is no pressure," he says quickly, "but there is

always food here for you."

It's my turn to be embarrassed, and I lean forward to press my face into the soft material of his t-shirt where it covers his shoulder. "Thanks, hon. When do you want to go to the shop?"

"We could leave just before nine," he says, taking a quick sip of his coffee. "Be there when it opens."

New plan. "Why don't we have breakfast here, before we go out?"

Dan nods. "Is that okay?"

"Yeah, why wouldn't it be?"

"You usually wait until—oh." He turns an accusing glare on me. "You usually wait until you are home and then *don't* eat, correct?"

I grimace. "Guilty."

Dan lets out a little sigh and presses a quick kiss to my forehead. "Of course we can eat here. Do you want to choose something? I will have a shower before we leave."

Our cosy, domestic morning is shaping up to be just perfect. This is a really good plan, and means I'll have more time when we're on campus to check everything for my exam, so I cuddle him for another few minutes while he finishes his coffee. I go to the kitchen and help myself to a bowl and grab the first box of cereal I find—cornflakes, unopened—and eat without thinking about it.

Good work, Will.

I'm helped along by how confident Dan seems all of a sudden. He lets me eat alone, so I don't feel like he's watching every mouthful, and wanders around in just a towel, tucked at his waist.

An incredible start to the day, if I'm honest.

I should probably start leaving a towel here. I have one with me in my overnight bag, but it seems silly to transport wet things each day. Maybe that's something we can talk about soon.

I peek out of his bedroom window while we're both getting dressed and quickly turn away. I had a bad feeling because of how bright the morning light was, but I just confirmed it.

I pull on my jumper from last night. It's cold out there.

"Nearly ready?" Dan asks, sneaking up behind me and making my heart flutter. For a moment, I consider not letting him open the curtain like he's about to.

"Yep," I say, holding my breath as he reaches past me to look out at the morning.

He groans.

The snow is a couple of inches thick across every surface. The sky is clear—for now—but it must have kept snowing through the night.

Dan looks like he's seen the end of the world.

I bite down laughter and cuddle him instead. My arms tie around his waist, tugging him towards me and making him let out a shocked little *oh*.

Eyes still fixed on the snow, Dan bites his lower lip and rests his arm over my shoulders. "Fuck."

I grin. He doesn't swear much, and he really sounds like he

means it. "Definitely making you buy gloves," I say, squeezing him. "Maybe some more layers."

"I do wear layers," he mutters. It's true. He's always got at least a t-shirt on under his jumper, and I'm sure he'd wear two pairs of trousers if he thought it would help.

"And a hat."

He groans again and pushes his face into my hair. "Okay, yes," he agrees. "Mostly I try to stay indoors."

"Can't do that *all* winter," I point out. "Snow is supposed to be *fun*."

"It isn't," he grumbles. "It's cold and wet and inconvenient."

"You're so *grumpy*," I tease, slipping one hand up under his jumper to press against his clean, warm t-shirt. "We barely ever get it here. Appreciate it."

He kisses my hair, loud and dramatic, and turns away from the window.

"Нет."

I laugh so much it hurts my stomach.

Eleven

Dan has a new SIM card by quarter past nine. By half past, we're on a bus together on the way to Keele and I've never enjoyed being on public transport so much. I sit by the window, eyes fixed on the road ahead of us, and do my best to avoid feeling sick.

"Kyphosis is curvature in which region of the spine?" Dan asks, reading from the list of saved questions on my phone.

"Thoracic," I say, like answering my name. "Lordosis is lumbar."

Dan rewards me with a quick kiss to my hair and another question, and we repeat this all the way through town until we're leaping out at the stop closest to my building.

Unsurprisingly, the snow hasn't melted. The pavements have been covered with grit, but the air is bitingly cold and Dan sneers.

"Grumpy," I say brightly, hooking my arm through his and leading him towards my room. "It's just *snow*. We'll warm up inside."

"I know." He sighs, lifting the corner of his mouth in a reluctant smile. "But I'm cold *now*."

I roll my eyes dramatically and make a big show of hurrying up so he doesn't have to be outside longer than necessary. It's a good plan, until we turn around the corner of my building and walk right into a snowball fight.

My first instinct is to double back and hide, but Dan surprises me. He sighs, laughs, and grabs my hand.

It's not just people from my building who have come out to blow off some revision stress. I recognise three people: Simon, who Dan and I have a habit of seeing in the corridor, and two others who I've seen in the kitchen and meekly introduced myself to. It looks like the three of them have formed a team against the others, and Simon waves us over.

I open my mouth to say *thanks but no thanks,* but Dan squeezes my hand and steps towards my flatmates. Okay. I glance up at him, trying to work out what he's thinking, and see nothing but a carefully measured neutral expression.

What does that mean?

"Join our team?" Simon asks, busying himself with scooping together handfuls of snow.

A snowball whizzes past us. I flinch towards Dan, as if I'm going to use him as a shield, and he just sighs.

"Five minutes?" Dan suggests, rubbing his thumb into the back of my hand. I'm so stunned that my mouth drops open. "Relax before your exam."

I don't need telling twice. I grin up at him, drop his hand,

and grab some fresh snow from the grass. This clearly marks me as an active participant, because an icy ball explodes against my shoulder and showers me in cold.

Dan laughs, loud and confident, and makes it all worth it.

"You're meant to be on *my* team," I say, lobbing my first snowball of the year generally in the direction of a group of people from the adjacent block. "Are you joining in? Or do you want the keys?"

Dan shoots me a sideways look and squats down next to me to grab his own handful of snow. "Five minutes," he repeats.

It's *awesome*.

Our group of five get absolutely covered in snow, but I think everyone playing does. Sometimes, Dan sees the snowballs coming and purposefully sticks his arm out or turns his back to block it for me. I give him a big smile each time he does this, too breathless to really say *thanks*, and he just laughs.

He laughs a *lot* during those five minutes.

When my hands are numb and Dan's nose is pinched red, I agree it's time to go inside. We each get a couple more throws in—I miss, but the snow Dan aims at the middle of someone's dripping wet hoodie lands perfectly—before retreating.

Simon follows us, breathless and jittery.

"We've been out there *ages*," he says, ducking as snow hits the brick wall near his head. My hands are cold and sluggish, so unlocking the door takes a moment longer than usual. "Good excuse to leave."

"You're welcome." I laugh, holding the door open for

them both to step through.

Dan shakes melted snow from his hair and Simon rushes straight to the kitchen.

"Do you want drinks?" he asks, pausing at the door. "I'm gonna make a hot chocolate so it's ready after a shower."

"That's a good idea," Dan says quietly. "You need to warm up."

"So do you," I hiss. Then louder so Simon can hear, "Yeah, why not. We'll just put our coats down."

Simon nods and grins at us. "See you in a sec."

We scurry to my room, which I unlock with a numb hand, and tumble into privacy for what feels like the first time all day.

My blinds are still down. This is a good thing.

"Can't believe you did that," I say, shrugging out of my coat and draping it over the back of my chair to dry.

Dan puts his on the hook behind my door and turns to face me with a tired but genuine smile.

My heart flutters.

"It was fun," he admits. "A nice break from work."

"Even though you got cold and wet?"

Dan sighs and steps right up to me so we're chest to chest. Being this close to him is still such a thrill. His hair is darkened by the wet snow and his nose and cheeks are still pinched red, showing where he's cold. It makes his eyes look even brighter, and his smile look warmer, and his cheekbones look sharper.

"Even though," he says.

I stretch up and kiss him. Where our faces touch he feels like ice, and I can only stand it for so many seconds before worry takes over.

"Let's get you warmed up," I whisper. "Coffee, then maybe a shower if you're still jittery, and then we're revising—"

"Or," Dan says, cutting me off with a quick kiss, "coffee, then we relax for an hour, then you have an early lunch, and then I walk you to your exam."

I frown at him. "I had breakfast."

"You did." He kisses my cheek. "Do you really think more revision today will help?"

I frown. "Doesn't hurt."

"Only if you're certain," Dan mutters. "We will take it steady."

"Fine. Coffee?"

With a little grunt deep in the back of his throat, Dan kisses me again.

This one's different. It's not short and sweet; it's low and warm and I'm glad people can't see in through my window. This kiss doesn't ask me to be patient. It doesn't want space, or for me to be slow.

I open my eyes, just to check. Dan's eyes are pressed shut and this close, I can see the very pale freckle which sits above his left cheekbone. It's like a little star and realising how lucky I am to be this close to him—to be trusted like this—makes my heart flutter.

Dan doesn't seem to want to stop. He lets go of one of my hands to hold my waist and tugs me closer.

Okay.

I close my eyes again and lean towards him. I've gone from shivering with cold to trembling with anticipation for wherever this kiss is taking us and I'm breathless.

We're supposed to be getting drinks.

There's only so long we can stand like this for. I'm stretched to reach him and it's not exactly comfortable, so I take a step back and inch us closer to my bed.

He gets it. His lips leave mine and brush against my cheek before we look at each other properly.

Dan's cheeks are still pink, but I don't think it's from the cold anymore.

"Okay?" I ask him, sitting down on the edge of my bed.

Dan kneels on the floor between my feet and my brain stops working.

What's he thinking? What's he doing?

"Okay," he echoes, both hands on my waist. "You?"

Does he expect me to be able to speak?

Fortunately for my embarrassment, Dan looks up at me and waits for my answer.

I nod.

He reaches up and kisses my jaw. It's nice. It's very nice, and I tip my head back to grin at the ceiling.

Dan's lips are dry—again—and scratch against my skin. It tickles, but in a strictly *this is enjoyable* way. Laughing is the last thing on my mind.

He hums, interrupting himself. "We were going to make drinks."

"Yeah," I sigh, "we were."

"Your friend will be expecting you in the kitchen."

I roll my eyes and catch his face between my hands. "Fine. But that was very fucking nice, and please feel welcome to kiss me like that whenever you want."

Dan grins up at me from the floor, eyes hazy and bright. "Maybe later."

I lift an eyebrow. "How am I supposed to concentrate on my exam now?"

He winks. *Winks.*

Fine.

I let go of him and he stands up, leaving me lightheaded. His fingertip lingers on the underside of my jaw where he's been kissing, and both of us are breathing more heavily than usual.

Is it a surprise? The adrenaline from the snowball fight is still fizzing through me and Dan's sparkling with electricity. Between us, we could probably power a couple of lightbulbs.

Instead, we go to the kitchen and spend a few minutes with Simon. Making small talk is difficult to begin with, especially with Dan smirking at me, but I do my very best.

I check the time when we get back to my room. It's quarter to eleven, so I have an hour before I have to start getting stressed about my exam.

We both sit on my bed with our warm mugs in our hands and our backs against the headboard. We haven't said anything alone since kissing, and I'm damned if I'm gonna be the first one to speak now.

Dan reaches past me to put his mug on the desk and I

catch fire.

He smells fucking amazing.

I think he can tell I'm holding my breath. I think he can hear the way my heart is thundering.

Dan's lips press against the side of my neck and I gasp up at the ceiling.

He's so gentle. His left hand cups my waist, but he supports himself with his right, pressed into the pillow between us. Like this, he's draped across me but putting no pressure through me—and I know I can stop him whenever I want.

I do not want to stop him.

I also don't want to push him, because I'm not sure how far he wants to take this, and because what he said about sex last night is still strong in my memory.

Dan kisses up to my cheek and stops, pulling back to look at me with his huge eyes. He's asking if I'm okay, and I reply with a broad smile.

There's every chance we'll just stare at each other for the next sixty minutes.

I kiss him, hoping to make it clear that I would very much like to do *more* than simply stare at him. I let my lips drop apart, almost begging him to kiss me *properly*, and close my eyes.

Dan responds. His nose presses against the side of mine and his hand creeps up my jumper, chilling against my skin.

"How are you *still* cold?" I mumble. I push my hands up his jumper and tug his t-shirt out the way. "Jesus, Dan."

He laughs and sits up, hitting me with a *look*. Completely winding me, he kicks off his shoes and gets under the duvet.

Okay. Okay.

The last person—the only person—I've had sex with is Lilley. Dan and I aren't going to change that today, but getting under the duvet with him while I'm feeling so electric is... brave.

I do it. I take my shoes off too, glance at the time, and cuddle him cautiously. I'm purposefully keeping space between our hips, but it's difficult when all I want to do is crush against him.

Dan takes my glasses from my face with his left hand and puts them on the desk next to our mugs. And then he pushes his fingers into my hair and kisses me again.

We kiss and we kiss and we kiss. I run my hands up and down Dan's chest; he plays with my hair and kisses my mouth, jaw, neck, shoulders...

It's a very good way of forgetting how nervous I am for my exam. It's a very good way of warming up, and I realise I'm looking for excuses to keep going when Dan's back to his usual temperature. We're warm and sweaty under the duvet and I would happily stay here for the rest of the day.

I don't want to stop. But I groan and turn my face away from his, panting for breath and aching all over. I feel like I've just been running.

"I should calm down before my exam," I mumble, jaw tired and sluggish. "Fuck."

Dan stops kissing and lies with his head on my chest

instead.

I try to stop breathing heavily so I don't jostle him, but it takes a moment. "I love you," I say. "I really love you."

He tightens his arm across my waist. "I love you." His voice is lower than usual, and I close my eyes, concentrating. "Are you okay? Was that okay?"

I groan and snuggle him into my chest. It's unusual for us to lie like this, and I want him to know I'm enjoying it. "Yes. That was *lovely* and you can do that whenever you want."

He's quiet. I know this means he's thinking about something, so I rub my hand gently against his arm and let my breathing come back to normal.

"Was that enough?"

I glare at the ceiling. "What do you mean, Dan?"

"Do you want me to make you orgasm?"

The absolute shock at hearing him ask such a question fortunately comes second to my understanding of *why* he's asking. Dan expects to have to give. It's who he is, but I blame Matthew for this particular uncertainty.

I fight down the surprise and the anger. Instead, I hold him tighter and answer confidently and clearly.

"No, darling."

I feel some of the tension leave his shoulders. "Are you sure?"

"Positive. This was really nice and I don't want anything *more*—not right now, at least." I bend awkwardly to kiss his hair. "Thank you for asking, but no."

Dan melts.

I don't think he expected such a firm answer. He sighs in relief and turns his face into my chest, nuzzling against my jumper. I keep my arms around his shoulders and cuddle him, giving him a chance to work out what he wants to do next.

"Okay," he says, sounding thin and light. "Okay. I believe you."

"As you should."

"But that was..."

I wait, drawing patterns into his shoulder with my fingertip while he chooses a word.

"Intense."

I laugh and shrug beneath him. "Yeah, it was. It was sexy. But that doesn't mean it has to lead to *sex*, y'know?"

Dan twists to blink up at me. For a moment, I think he's going to spill some big and horrible story about his relationship with Matthew. I brace myself, ready to support and protect him however he needs, and cup his face in my hand.

"Thank you," he says. "Спасибо. I feel safe with you."

"You big, tall silly," I whisper. "You're *welcome*. It's all fine. I'm very happy right now—are you?"

Beaming, he nods.

"There we go." I twirl his hair between my fingers. "I feel very peaceful and loved."

Dan closes his eyes. I'd love to let him fall asleep on me, but I do need to get ready for my exam.

"I love you, William," he whispers. "This is a good day."

My heart jumps. After yesterday—and being plagued by those texts from Matthew—and the last week or so, I have to agree. Today is good.

Nonetheless—

"Let's wait until after my exam before we decide that," I say, nervousness flipping the edge of my voice. "Can you read more questions to me?"

I was expecting him to protest, but he smiles and sits up. I miss the weight of him instantly.

"Drinks," he says. Damn it. We forgot them, and he takes them out to the kitchen to microwave without really giving me a choice.

I don't need the hot chocolate to warm me up now, but I appreciate that he probably does need the caffeine in his coffee. Especially if he's going to spend this afternoon studying.

While he's out of the room, I double-check my pencil case. Calculator, pens, pencils, ruler. My student identification card is in my wallet, which I add to the pile. Then I just need my glasses. Ready.

A trickle of anticipation runs through me just before Dan comes back into my bedroom.

"You want to cook tonight?"

Oh, damn. I did say that.

"Any ideas?"

"None," I admit. "You?"

He hums and sits on his side of the bed. "No. I might go to the shop while you're taking your exam."

"Not a bad idea." I sit beside him again and reluctantly take my mug. "Can you quiz me?"

Dan glares at me over his coffee. "Drink first," he says. "We can count it as your lunch. I know you won't eat anything."

Blushing, because he's exactly right, I drink in silence.

Dan slips his arm low around my back and holds on to me while he drains his mug. It's comfortable and reassuring and I can hardly believe it's still morning. Haven't we done enough today?

"Pass me your phone," Dan whispers as soon as I've finished my hot chocolate. "Ready for some questions?"

"Always," I say, giving him the phone and putting my mug down at the same time. I settle in against his chest, close my eyes to concentrate, and we spend the next half hour revising.

Twelve

It's snowing again by the time we leave to walk to my exam. Dan sighs, pops a piece of gum in his mouth, and hides his hands in his pockets.

I'm jittering. I don't think it's just from the cold.

"Talk me through it," Dan says, setting a fast enough pace that I don't feel like we're dawdling. I'm going to be at my exam room way early, but that's better than being late.

"I'll be fine," I say, trying to make myself believe it. "I know enough. All I've got to do is keep my brain organised and stay relaxed, right?"

Dan smiles at me. "Right. You know everything you need, darling."

I do. I'm sure I do. And yet there's a heavy lump in my throat. I'm clutching my pencil case, fingers drumming nervously against the clear plastic, and I could do with a hug. Dan's trying to keep warm, though, and I don't want to stop us walking.

I don't need to worry about that. For reasons I can't imagine, Lilley and Cassie are walking towards us from the direction of the medical building. They're holding hands and, for the shortest moment, I'm sad that Dan and I aren't touching.

"Hey!" Cas calls, dragging Lilley towards us.

Lil rolls her eyes and drags her feet a little, but I see the way she tightens her hold on her girlfriend's hand.

"It's your first exam, right?"

I nod.

"Thought we'd come and say good luck."

Before I can say anything, Cas throws her free arm around me and nearly sends me flying.

I clutch my pencil case to my chest but laugh, surprised and happy about it.

"You'll smash it," Cas whispers before letting me go again. "Have you spoken to Peter today?"

Why would she ask that? Some of the happiness fades, replaced with grey, and I glance up at Dan as if he's going to explain why my best friend hasn't contacted me recently. His expression is blank.

"Nah," I say, trying and failing to sound like I don't care. "Have—have you?"

Cas shrugs. "A little bit."

I don't like this.

I turn to Dan again, searching for reassurance, when I see a couple of guys in the corner of my eye. They're rushing towards us from the direction of the SU, hand in hand.

Peter and Anthony stumble to a stop next to us. Cassie is

grinning like she's won something, Lilley is laughing at me, and Dan just winks. Damn him.

I groan at the sky. "You're all so smug."

"Knew you'd be stressed," Peter says, smiling a dimpled grin. "But you're gonna smash it, so we thought we'd all go out for dinner this evening. Celebrate your first exam, y'know?"

I—what?

"I knew," Dan reassures me, taking one hand out of his pocket to push my hair away from my glasses. My stomach does its usual flip. "I know you wanted to cook, but we can do that tomorrow."

I grin at him. "Fine."

Peter laughs and grabs me for a hug. Okay, this is a welcome distraction. I don't need to go into my exam feeling like I'm going to be sick. I need to be steady and calm and grounded.

"Wasn't sure if you'd hate it or not," Peter admits. "You're a busy guy."

I shrug and hug him back for the briefest moment. "Yeah, but this is nice. You know I love spending time with you all."

Anthony is staying noticeably quiet.

"What are you doing while he's kicking ass this afternoon?" Lilley asks, aiming the question at Dan.

Peter lets go of me and I lean straight into my boyfriend's arm, seeking more cuddles.

He answers while wrapping his arm around my shoulders, understanding, without even making eye contact with me, that I want to be held together. "Library. I need to study."

"We could sit with you," Lilley suggests, dark green eyes flashing between us. "If you don't want to be alone. We've got work to do anyway."

How is she so good? If I'm honest, the thought of leaving Dan alone this afternoon *has* been setting my teeth on edge. He's really giving quitting smoking a good shot, but he's had me watching him all day. I still feel terrible about saying *you of all people,* and I bet he's thinking about it too. It's not the sort of thing you can just brush off. I'm not sure how to fix it.

And sure, we've got him a new phone number, but what if Matthew comes to campus to find him?

What if Matthew comes to campus to find him?

The thought fills me with terror but before it can manifest as a scream, Dan speaks.

"I would appreciate that, thank you," he says. "Matthew is out of the hospital."

Lilley and Cassie share a worried glance.

"So, I'd rather have company. Peter and Anthony were already joining me."

"And you *didn't* think to tell me?" I groan, glaring up at him. I'm so relieved I could melt.

"Wanted seeing them to be a surprise," Dan whispers, smiling down at me. "Stop stressing."

"You know I can't just do that."

"No, because you're a big puddle of *worry*," Peter says, nudging me before falling sideways into Anthony's arms. "We've got this. All you gotta do is smash this exam."

I purse my lips. "Sure."

"You'll be fine," Cas says. "We'll all stick together and find you in two hours, all right?"

Two hours. All I've got to do is survive the next two hours—and trust my friends will keep Dan safe.

I'm being ridiculous. Dan is more than capable of keeping himself safe. The bruise across his eyebrow is still eye-catching, and the cut put there by the glass Matthew threw at him is still covered in a scab, but he smiles naturally. He's confident. He's safe.

"Promise me you'll be okay." I sigh, looking at him over the top of my glasses. We're too close for me to really look properly.

"Я обещаю," he says.

This may be the first time the others have heard him speak in Russian. I'm glowing with pride and grin up at him, suddenly confident that, between us, we can do anything. Because we can, right? He can recover from a drug addiction and escape an abusive relationship. I can pass my second-year exams and progress to level five. Dan can pass all of his third-year exams in one go and get a job—

I stop there. Thinking about how difficult it's going to be for him to find a job is nauseating, and exactly the opposite of what I need right now.

"We'll get two hours of intensive revision done," Lilley says firmly, "and come and grab you after. It'll be early for dinner, but maybe we could take over one of the study rooms and prat about for a bit."

I laugh and look away from Dan. He takes the opportunity to press a kiss into my hair and I forget what I was going to say.

"They're gonna be disgusting," Cas stage-whispers. "Sure you want to invite Will and Dan along?"

Lil sighs dramatically and offers Cas a red-lipped smirk. "They're better than the other two."

I'd actually managed to ignore the way Peter and Anthony have their hands in each other's back pockets.

I notice someone from my classes walk into the building and suddenly, the reality of the moment hits. I've got to go and answer anatomy questions.

Dan tugs me closer and kisses my hair again. "You're fine," he whispers. "Want us to leave?"

"No." But they need to. I need to go and find my seat. "Promise you'll find me after?"

"We'll be right here," Cas says, tucking her hair back behind her ear. "Do you think you'll leave early?"

A strange quirk of university exams: you can actually walk out early. If you've done enough, or think you simply can't get any more done, you can just...leave.

"Absolutely not," I say, half-laughing. "I'm gonna need every second they give me."

Dan catches my right hand very suddenly and cradles it between his. "Should have made you wear gloves," he mutters, rubbing warmth into my fingers. "Are you okay?"

I sigh and raise an eyebrow. "Yeah. Get yourselves gone so I can go indoors."

Lilley and Cassie get the message. Lil starts walking,

throwing me a quick grin, and drags Cas away.

"Just think of me there, telling you all the answers!" Cassie calls, stumbling over her feet.

"You know you've got this," Peter says, bumping me with his fist. He keeps glancing up at Dan like he wants to say something to him but doesn't know what. "Proud of you."

Ah, crap.

"Thanks," I say. "I mean it."

Peter winks. "I know, I know. We're wonderful. Come on, babe."

Anthony smiles at me. It's a warm, honest smile but he, unlike Peter, can't even look at Dan. Interesting. Annoying.

"Good luck," Anthony says, letting Peter lead him after Cas and Lil.

Dan and I have a final moment together and I take a long, deep breath.

"Steady," he murmurs, sweeping me into his arms. I clutch my pencil case tighter again. "I love you. I'm proud of you. I'll be fine. Lilley wouldn't let anything happen, would she?"

I laugh at that and shake my head. No, Lilley certainly wouldn't let anything happen to Dan. Not after seeing him on Friday.

I can't start thinking about the way he trembled as we ran away from Matthew—

"I've got you," Dan whispers, lips by my ear. "I love you. Two hours, darling. Then I won't let go of you until the next exam."

"Is that a promise?"

"Prometo."

I pull back to look at him. "That was new."

He's blushing again and smirks. "Variety. Spanish this time."

I *glow* with pride. "You know, I did Spanish in high school."

He cocks his head. "Did you?"

"Not very well, but yeah."

Dan laughs and kisses my cheek, warm and purposeful beneath my glasses. "Te amo. Buena suerte."

"I will *die*."

He laughs again and lets go of me, nudging me gently towards the building. "Please, no. Just be brilliant."

I grin and watch him go. I should have told him I love him back, but I guess I'll have to make up for that when we get home tonight.

For now, I embrace how warm his whispering makes me feel and I concentrate on my first exam of the season.

Thirteen

My hand aches, my thoughts are void of anything coherent, and my mouth is dry as I leave the exam room. My classmates are all in a similar state of shock.

"It went...well," I hear one bravely say. "Like, I didn't struggle."

"Maybe we've actually got good teachers," Miley says, laughing. We sit together sometimes in lectures. "Plot twist."

"Do you wanna meet up on Friday?" I ask, surprising all of us. "Revise for next week."

Miley grins. "Sounds good to me. Library at nine?"

Stomach full of butterflies, I agree. So do three others: the brave and surprised one, who I *think* is called Grace; a guy who's even quieter than me who I think is called Sebastian; and another guy who's as tall as Dan and is called Jesse. All of them intimidate me—even quiet Sebastian—but we're having a moment here. We're sharing something.

We can do this.

Maybe, in about three years' time, we'll be graduating together. Maybe we'll be on placements together. Maybe we'll end up on rotations at the same place, or even working together.

Whatever. We can do this.

We all power our phones back on from their two hours of enforced peace and wait while notifications flick through. When we're all ready, we set up a group chat and promise each other we'll confirm again after tomorrow's exam. Tomorrow is the first of the one-on-one exams and we're all a bit nervous about it. To say the least.

All organised, our little group disperses and I look up.

Miley looks over her shoulder at me and waves, but my eyes go straight to Dan.

He's fidgety. He wants to be smoking, but he wouldn't dare when he's surrounded by Lilley, Cassie, Peter, and Anthony.

I march straight to him, and he holds his arms open.

"Did it go well?" Cas laughs, stepping back as I fly past and launch myself at Dan.

He sweeps me up and we do a half turn so Dan's back is to the rest of them. "Are you okay?" he asks, voice low and urgent. "Was it okay?"

"Yeah, it was good. It was great." I laugh and tighten my arms around his neck. "You okay?"

"Yeah. You looked drained," he explains, letting me put my feet back on the ground and holding me steady. "Promise it went okay?"

I pull back and grin at him. "Yes, Dan. It went okay."

The others take this as their cue to start babbling.

"You looked like you were gonna throw up," Cassie says.

"He *always* does."

"Thanks, Lil," I mutter.

"Was the exam all right?" Peter asks, frowning at me. "Convince me."

"It was fine." I laugh. "Better than fine—scarily easy."

"Show off," Dan mutters, low and soft in my ear. His arms are around my waist, hands held gently together over one of my hips. It's protective, intimate, and so lovely I could cry.

"Were they your course friends?" Cas asks, nodding back at where I stood with the little group.

I shrug. "I wouldn't say *friends*, but maybe one day."

"I'm glad," Dan whispers.

Lilley grins at me. "So it went well? We don't need to do an *it will all be okay* rescue party?"

I roll my eyes. "Nah. We're gonna meet up on Friday to revise for next week."

Dan's arms tighten and he presses a kiss into my hair. "Good."

I knew he'd like this. It's a *lot* to ask him to support all of my revision, especially while he's trying so hard to study for his own exams.

"Wanna go and sit somewhere?" Peter asks. "It's fucking cold."

"It is," Dan says quickly. "Can we go back to the library?"

"Good plan." Peter starts walking straightaway. "We can

grab drinks from the machine and play hangman or something."

We follow them and Dan reluctantly lets go of me so we can walk holding hands. He takes my pencil case for me and stashes it in one of his big coat pockets.

"What is *hangman*?" he whispers.

I grin up at him. "Word game. You think of a word, mark how many letters are in it, and everyone else has to guess."

Dan tuts. "I know it. Sounded weird when Peter said it."

Lilley leans over. "That's because Peter thinks it's *fun* and it is *not*."

"Dan's great with word games," I warn, squeezing his hand. "Brace yourself."

Lilley groans. "Great. So we've got an English student *and* a linguistics nerd."

"Anyone know what Anthony's doing?" Cas asks, swinging Lilley's hand. "He's barely talked to me."

"Something with philosophy," Dan says.

We all look up at him, wondering how on Earth he knows this.

Realising we need an explanation, he continues. Eyes forward, fixed on the library, and hand tight around mine. "He was on the same course as Matthew, but two years behind."

I don't know how to respond. I remember Matthew knew Anthony through football, but there's a dark undercurrent to what Dan just said.

"How did you meet Matthew, Dan?" Lilley asks, and I nearly reach over to thump her.

"He was doing politics and philosophy," he says without missing a beat. "Dual honours. I know he met Anthony while he was waiting for lectures, and they recognised each other from football."

"Never understood people studying philosophy," Lilley mutters. "What a waste of money."

"It's interesting," Cas says. "Feeds into how we learn everything else, right?"

Lil hums. "Maybe. But do you need three years of it? Really?"

I let them discuss the apparent pros and cons of studying a degree in philosophy and turn all of my attention to Dan. My shock from leaving the first exam so confidently has worn off now. And I'm pulling things together, using what I know about Dan's tendency to leave out the most important parts of a story, and make him stop walking.

Lilley and Cassie keep going until they've joined Peter and Anthony at the foot of the steps outside the library. They wait there for us without making it look obvious.

"What else?" I ask, looking up at Dan.

He sighs and looks away.

"Dan? I know there's something—"

"It's okay," he whispers. "Anthony doesn't need to know I know. Okay?"

I nod firmly. "Promise. Just us."

Dan looks around us, checking for anyone who might overhear. We're blocking the path, but there's no one around. It's pretty clear, really, that we're having an intense conversation. We're chest to chest, clinging to each other's hands, and a bomb could go off right now, but I wouldn't notice. I'm prepared for anything Dan could possibly tell me.

"They slept together in the first week," Dan whispers. "Just once, I think. It was before Anthony even met Peter, so I don't know if he knows—I don't know if he *needs* to know."

There's a rock in my chest.

"Matthew showed me pictures of them together."

"*What*?" I hiss, tugging Dan's hands to my chest.

He blinks slowly and looks at me, pretty eyes sad and tired. "It was not the first time."

"Dan—"

"Anthony doesn't need to know we know," he says. "Promise—"

"Of course. I won't tell anyone, hon."

His shoulders relax. "Thank you. Can we talk about it later? It doesn't matter now, and I don't want us to be upset this afternoon. You've done well, and you have another exam tomorrow."

I grunt. "Yeah. True. Are you okay, though? What was it like spending the afternoon with him?"

Dan raises an eyebrow at me. "I'm fine, darling. I'm fine. It doesn't upset me, but I realised you should know."

I nod and bring his hands to my lips to kiss. "Okay. Thank you for telling me, Dan."

He frees one hand to sweep his fingers through my hair, playing with the curls and twisting them away from my face. It makes me smile.

"I love you," he says. "Thank you for not turning this into a big thing."

"Love you too." I grin into his knuckles as I say it, temporarily overwhelmed with how very true it is. I *love* him. "So proud of you."

I don't need to look up to know he just raised an eyebrow. Instead, I laugh and twist his hand so I can slide our fingers together. I bump my forehead into his arm, hoping he knows this means I'd be hugging him if we were somewhere more comfortable, and lead him along the slush-covered path to my friends.

To *our* friends.

Awkwardness with Anthony aside, I think Lilley and Cas are definitely Dan's friends now. Peter is too—even though I think we have work to do if we want to trust each other again. Realising I've built a wall between myself and my best friend makes my chest feel heavy, but he greets us with a smile. No sly comment about us being all over each other.

Maybe Peter's grown up over the last couple of weeks.

We climb the steps together in three groups of two. I only realise now how perfect this set up is. We're balanced. We're unanimously in love. No part of me is worried about what will happen when people realise Dan and I are dating, because there's nothing to single us out. Lilley and Cassie are all over each other. Peter and Anthony are all over each other. We'd be noticeable if we *weren't* holding hands, to be honest.

We scan our cards and let ourselves into the busy, steamy library. The foyer always reminds me of swimming pools. The humidity is outrageous and even the staff at the desk look like they're about to give you a locker key.

"Let's try this floor before we torture ourselves with more stairs," Lilley says, leading the way to the first open area of tables, seats, and bookcases. Lining the window are so-called silent-study desks, where you're encouraged to wear earphones and keep your mouth shut. Metal bookcases from the fifties fill the middle of the room, then low coffee tables and settees with ripped corners sit in clusters against the wall. Some of these clusters are centred around whiteboards, but they're all in use.

It is revision season, after all.

We walk as quietly as we can until we reach the far end of the room where there's a door leading to a corridor lined with more doors. Each of these holds a private study room and if we magically find one which isn't booked, we're winning.

Lilley leads the way, pausing briefly at each door to read the printed timetable. She stalks away from each one with an irritated tut, but I realise when we reach the end of the corridor that I don't actually care. I'm enjoying this time spent drifting around campus with my friends.

"New plan." Lilley sighs, one arm wrapped tight around the front of her waist. "Any objections to the SU?"

There are none. We've seemed to agree there's no point looking at the rest of the study spaces and we go back to the outdoors steps.

Dan groans.

It's snowing.

I laugh, bump against his arm again, and drag him down the steps. The others follow, holding the cold handrails just in case, and we regroup at the top of the path that leads to the Students' Union.

Dan looks miserable.

"What's wrong with you?" Lilley asks him, dark eyebrows pulled together. Her skin is even paler in the snow, and she and Cas look like they could be sapphic vampires here to kill the rest of us.

Dan groans and holds his free hand out to catch a snow-flake. "I hate the cold."

Peter gawks. "But you're *Russian*."

"Told you," I say. "Everyone thinks Russians love the snow, babe."

"Not this one," Dan says darkly. He wipes his hand on the side of his coat and gives me a tired, apologetic smile. "I should have bought gloves. You're right."

"At least you have a decent coat." I cling to his arm, empha-sising how much padding is between me and him. "You're just a big baby."

Dan rolls his eyes and tugs me into a very sudden hug. It's so strong and unexpected that I'd fall over—if he weren't holding me with all of his strength. He growls lightly, teasingly in my ear. "You are insufferable," he whispers. "Baby? Fine. Take me somewhere warm and buy me a drink."

Help.

Light-headed, red-hot, and speechless, I stare up at him. Right now, I'd do anything he asked.

He sees just how utterly ruined I am and smirks, well aware of his ability to dazzle. It's all over for me. Dan is absolutely radiant with unrestrained love and, when he kisses me, my thoughts go completely blank.

I forget who I am, where I am, and that my friends are currently gawking at us.

Dan takes a tight handful of the back of my coat and holds me in place, kissing me like he doesn't care we're in the centre of campus.

"Tag your porn, Dan." Lilley groans.

We slip apart. My heels hit the floor and Dan stands up to almost his full height, pink-cheeked and smug as hell.

Holy crap. Maybe we should go back to my room for a bit.

"Baby," I whisper, so quietly the others might not hear.

Dan cocks his head and delicately touches his cold fingertips to my jaw.

I think he's going to kiss me again and I can't believe I'm having such a public and heated display of affection when he leans in and puts his lips to my ear.

"I love you," he murmurs. "And it is because I love you that I'm doing this."

"Doing wh—?"

His hands drop from my face and he grabs me by the waist to lift me.

I scream, breaking off in a laugh, and hold him so tight it hurts.

"Time for coffee," Dan announces. He carries me down the path to the SU, leading our friends, and no doubt draws the attention of everyone within sight.

I don't care. I'm embarrassed, yeah, but Dan is laughing under his breath and it's so clear he's feeling good. He's happy. He's relaxed, he's flirting, and he's proud to be seen in love with me. I would take this over anything. If someone had told me that telling Dan I love him would result directly in this moment, *I'm bi* would have been my next words.

Okay, that's an exaggeration. It would always be difficult. I think it's always going to be difficult, but having Dan's arms around me makes it a little bit easier. Having Dan whisper *I love you* in my ear makes being out feel a little bit safer. Having his arms so shamelessly around me makes being out feel like the right choice.

I close my eyes in relief.

"You okay?" Dan asks when the ground levels out.

We still have steps to deal with, and I start to wriggle, expecting to be let down.

"Oh, not yet."

"I'm fine—I can walk, Dan—"

"I don't want to let go of you," he admits. "You're warm."

I laugh again and hide my face right in his neck. He smells amazing.

"Do you think I embarrassed Lilley?" Dan asks, walking down the steps with no problems at all. "Did I embarrass you?"

"Definitely embarrassed Lil," I say. "And *definitely* embarrassed me. I loved it, though."

"Did you?"

"*Obviously.*"

He chuckles and presses a breathless kiss to my hair.

We reach the SU. With a little sigh, Dan lowers me back to the floor and lets me stand again.

"Thank you," I say, trying to regain some sort of dignity.

It's a pointless effort: Lilley and Peter are laughing so much they might faint, and Dan looks like he's won the world.

"Пожалуйста," he whispers.

"Okay, you're a flirt *and* a show-off," Lilley says, sweeping past us to open the door to the SU. "Tall, handsome, smart—"

"Patient to hang out with Will for so long," Cassie adds.

"Rude."

Dan kisses my hair again and holds the door.

Peter and Anthony follow us in, both of them still laughing.

"Will's buying drinks then, yeah?" Lil asks, throwing herself down at a table as soon as it's vacated. Finally, we have somewhere to sit. "Latte please, hon."

I roll my eyes. "Fine. What does everyone else want? It's a good job I brought my money, isn't it?"

Dan refuses to sit down with the others. I take their orders, leave my coat on a chair to claim it, and wait patiently for my boyfriend to explain why he's suddenly so clingy.

He waits until I've placed our six-drink order.

"I don't want either of us to be alone for the rest of the day," he admits, one hand gently resting on my waist from behind while we wait. Like this, we're both facing the same way. "Don't panic—"

"I promise."

He rubs his thumb against my shirt. "I saw him."

Ah, shit.

I guess I knew it would happen, but I'd hoped it wouldn't be today. Not this week. Not when I have to leave Dan alone while I sit in another exam tomorrow. Not after last night, when he had such a horrible panic attack—

I take a breath. "Where and when?"

"Outside the library, when we left to find you. He looked straight at me."

"How do you feel?" I swear, I'm ready to run across the entire campus and find that man. I could kill him for everything he's done to Dan.

"I'm okay," Dan says. "I'm surprised. I thought I would be upset, or scared, but I'm okay. Having everyone there helped."

Once again, I'm incredibly grateful for my friends.

"He just looked at me and walked away," he whispers. "Like he slightly recognised me. He didn't try to talk to me."

"Good," I mutter. "Are you sure you're okay?"

"Yeah."

"Are you okay with staying out, or do you want to go back to mine?"

He pulls me closer. "I'm okay. I think I'm relieved."

"Relieved?"

"I saw him and nothing happened," he explains.

Okay, I agree: it's a relief.

"I think he was probably still watching us when we found you."

I lean my head back, into his arm. This goes a long way to explaining Dan's clinginess. "Did any of the others see him?"

"Not sure."

I take a gentle breath. I suppose this is our best-case scenario. Dan hasn't crumbled and he hasn't disappeared and he hasn't got angry. He's just...here.

Maybe he's in shock.

But he was overflowing with happiness and joy a few minutes ago. Was that him trying to overcompensate for however seeing Matthew made him feel?

I twist and look up at him. There's nothing suspicious— no tell-tale mask, no tense eyebrows or locked jaw. He just looks like Daniel, happy to be here and waiting for me to explain why I'm staring at him.

"Out of ten," I say, "how much do you want a cigarette?"

He laughs. "Eleven."

I groan.

"Maybe eight," he corrects, touching my forehead very briefly with his fingertips. *Stop frowning*. "We should have bought more gum."

That's an easy fix. "They'll have some in the pharmacy here," I say. "Next one. Out of ten, how anxious do you feel?"

He shrugs and surprises me. "One."

"Really?"

"If we ignore how much I miss cigarettes," he says, "yes. I feel peaceful."

I speak quickly, before I can chicken out of it. "Even though you saw Matthew?"

He nods. "Yes. I'm happy. There was closure."

Before I can say anything else, our order gets called. We balance the six hot cups between us, check we're both okay, and go over to our table.

Cas is sitting on Lilley's lap.

Lil sees me smirking and sticks out her tongue. "Chair shortage," she explains, taking her latte from me. "Thanks, Will."

"Welcome."

Cas has a green tea, Peter has white coffee, and Anthony has a latte too.

Dan puts my hot chocolate—I don't think I've ever had so much sugar in one day, but never mind—and his coffee on the table, sits on the chair holding my coat, and tugs me down onto his lap.

I should have expected that.

The others laugh, but it's so natural and comfortable that we don't really turn it into a big thing.

Lilley and Cas are already cosy.

Peter and Anthony are holding hands on the table, like separating would be physically painful for them.

I'm glad my best friend has found someone to love. When I see them together like this, I start to realise just how confusing this last semester must have been for Peter. Guilt for ditching him for Dan aches in my chest and I want to apologise again—but now isn't the right time.

I lean into Dan's chest, getting comfy, and try something else.

"You two look so happy," I say, aiming it at Peter and Anthony. I could have said the same to Lil and Cas, but they don't need affirmation. "Are things okay?"

Peter grins at me, dimples in his cherub face and teeth so bright they nearly blind me.

But it's Anthony who speaks, and I think this is a really good sign.

"I've never been happier," he says, voice soft. "I'm just *relaxed*. Like it doesn't take any effort."

I can't help but smile.

"Speaking of effortless," Lilley says, "are we gonna talk about how Dan just *carried* you across campus?"

I blush. I'm sure Dan's blushing too, but I can't twist to look at him.

"He is so small it's easy," Dan says, blasé. "You are not very heavy."

Unease settles on my tongue like a bad taste. "I ate breakfast," I mumble, unreasonably defensive. "It's not my fault you're so damn tall."

Dan kisses my hair and wraps his arms more firmly around me, cuddling me to him. "You did," he says, "and you're doing well. But you *are* small."

"You're shorter than Cas," Lilley points out. "And that's impressive."

"Rude," Cassie mutters, dropping a kiss to her girlfriend's cheek. "You're just tall."

"I don't think I like this," I say darkly. "I buy you all drinks and you immediately start attacking me—"

"It's not an attack," Lil says. "It's just the truth."

I stick out my tongue at her.

"Watch out, Dan. He's feisty."

Peter snorts with laughter and takes the lid off his cup, letting the steam out. "Pretty sure you have the crown for *feisty*, Lil."

Lilley winks, more than happy to take that title.

I very accidentally close my eyes.

It's busy in the SU. People are having mid-afternoon coffee breaks, like us, and we were lucky to get four seats and a table. The bustle of university life hums around me while my friends laugh at each other and, in Dan's arms, I fall asleep.

Just for a few minutes. I think.

When I open my eyes again, I'm still cradled into Dan's chest and the others are still talking. I have my face turned into his neck and it's sheltered, like I could be anywhere in the world. I nearly just go back to sleep.

"Your drink is still warm," Dan murmurs, voice rumbling through me like a lullaby. "Do you want it?"

I hum and cling to him, asking for another few minutes. I haven't quite come back into the real world yet. My thoughts aren't lining up, and I keep jumping between exam questions and the imagined face I've assigned to Matthew and the realisation that, this time tomorrow, I'll have done my first ever clinical exam.

Each time that last thought hits me, I hold my breath.

Maybe I should be studying.

I have the Student Room discussion page saved as a tab on

my phone. Without giving an explanation—or reaching for my drink—I pull out my phone and groggily navigate to the tab. My eyes are barely open, but I start reading an entry from last year—even though I've already nearly memorised it—just to reassure myself that I know what to expect.

Dan takes my phone from me and puts it face-down on the table.

Stunned, I sit up away from his shoulder. The others have stopped talking and are looking at us, like they're expecting some sort of eruption, but he's far too correct for me to argue.

All I'm doing by forcing myself to study immediately after waking up is stressing myself out. Although I want to say it soothed some of the stress, I should have at least had my drink. I should have at least said something.

Dan's patiently waiting with one eyebrow raised and I realise something else too.

The world is blurry and it's not just because I'm still half asleep. He took my glasses off for me.

"Thank you," I whisper, cheeks red. "I needed that."

Smug, Dan nods.

"You okay, Will?" Cassie asks, reaching over to touch my arm. "You just passed out."

I half laugh. I'd hoped they hadn't noticed. "Yeah. Burned out from the exam, I think."

"And you thought a good idea was to revise again," Dan mutters, touching the side of his thumb to the tip of my nose. It's a gentle, adoring chastisement, and I totally deserve it. "Silly."

"Oops."

Dan rolls his eyes but smiles, satisfied I understand why he stopped me.

I'm grateful for it, I really am. I grab my drink, hoping this earns me another few hours without being nagged about food, and relax again when he snakes his arms around my waist.

"You look exhausted," Peter says. "Would you be better off having a couple of hours in your room? We can come and get you when we get hungry."

Tempting. But I really am enjoying this time with my friends, and I have a feeling Dan would make a valid point about me needing to let my brain relax. The revision I did for today's exam will help me for tomorrow—and it's not like I haven't been working on tomorrow's exam. Anything I do now will just be to reassure myself I know enough and can make the links between test results and symptoms to causes, and I can do that anywhere.

"Nah," I say. "Dan's right. I need to take it easy for a few hours."

Peter actually looks worried about me. "If you need to sleep—"

"'I won't sleep tonight if I do," I point out. "Maybe we should get snacks or something."

Dan does a very, very good job of acting like this isn't the first time he's ever heard me suggest I eat more than just meals. I feel the way he holds his breath, but the others don't notice.

"Good idea," Lilley says, looking over my head at Dan. Okay, they both know. They know me better than anyone else in the world. "Shall we go and grab a selection?"

Cassie nods and hops to her feet, taking the opportunity to stretch. "You're bony," she mutters, shrugging into her warm coat and quickly checking for her purse. "Might have to swap when we get back."

"I'll squish you," Lilley warns.

"That's fine by me."

They leave without giving us a chance to offer suggestions and a big slice of regret wedges itself in my stomach. I want to trust that Lilley has an accurate idea of the sort of thing I could snack on, but Cassie might lead her astray.

I pick my phone up and let Dan watch the screen while I send a hasty message to Lil.

15:32 Will: something like fruit would be really nice!

15:33 Lil: something LIKE fruit? Not actual fruit but LIKE fruit?

15:34 Will: don't be a dick
15:34 Will: but if all you bring back are crisps and sweets I'll cry

15:34 Lil: noted x

Dan kisses my hair when I put my phone down again. And

then he says something that nearly makes me choke.

"Did you see Matthew earlier?" he asks, aiming it at Anthony.

Peter and I hold our breath and share a glance.

"No," Anthony says, eyes wide and terrified. "What? Does this mean you did? When—where was he?"

Dan nods and keeps me cuddled close. Was he waiting for an opportunity to talk about this away from Lilley and Cas? It makes me a little bit sad to think he doesn't feel comfortable around them, but I get it. Matthew is a problem Dan and Anthony share, and we don't need to bring more people into this nightmare.

"Before we found William," Dan says. Not the time to think about how lovely it is to hear my full name. "He saw us all and walked away."

"Fuck." Peter sighs. "How did he look?"

"Bad," Dan admits. "Worse than I did."

Oh, hello. Are we talking about Dan's recovery? I sit up a little straighter and take a tight handful of his jumper so we can't be separated.

Anthony grimaces. "Maybe I should have gone to see him—"

"No," Peter and I say at the same time.

Dan squeezes me. "He has the help he needs," Dan says. "I am surprised he hasn't been kept somewhere."

I think quickly. "You expected him to go to rehab?"

Dan shrugs. "It would be easier for him. He must have friends supporting him—and he must have found somewhere to live. He could not continue with university."

I make sure to commit each syllable to memory. "What makes you say that, hon?" I ask, watching his face for any of those signs of stress I'm so used to seeing on him.

He curls his lip. "He was *bad*, William," he whispers, as if he's forgotten our audience. "Bad. I do not know if he will stay clean."

Peter and I share a quick look.

"How does that make you feel?" I ask, sounding like a shitty psychiatrist. But I need to know.

Dan flashes a smile at me. "Glad I left him," he admits. "But worried. I hope he has help, but it's not safe for any of us to *provide* help. Do you understand?"

That question is aimed at Anthony, who nods. He looks queasy.

I remember something from October, when I was anxiously researching opiate addiction treatment. "I assume he's on a replacement like—" I almost say *like you are*, but I don't feel comfortable voicing that in front of Anthony. I say, "Like buprenorphine," instead.

Dan nods. "I assume so."

"It might be that they aren't letting him take it at home."

I've completely lost Peter and Anthony, but this is more for Dan's benefit. I can't have him worrying Matthew is going through this recovery alone.

"He probably has to see a pharmacist each day," I say. "That way they control how much he has *and* he's forced to check in at least once every twenty-four hours. If you think he would struggle so badly to take responsibility for his own prescription, I'm sure the hospital realised too. They wouldn't let him disappear."

I feel the way Dan relaxes. "This makes sense," he whispers. "It was an option for me."

My stomach twists. "Why didn't you go for it?"

"I was not *as* bad," he murmurs, defensive. "And I needed to be independent so I could leave for my VISA."

Do you think Peter and Anthony would mind if I completely ignored them for the next hour? Never mind me needing to go to my room; I want to wrap Dan up in a big, warm blanket and protect him from the world.

"You smashed it," I whisper. "But this is my point. You said Matthew would struggle more. There's no way they'll be letting him go home with a box of opioid painkillers, is there?"

The logic works. Dan nods, smiles, and presses a quick kiss to my cheek. "You are so smart," he whispers. "Thank you."

Satisfied, and blushing very slightly, I turn back to Anthony. "He'll be fine," I say, even though it sucks to be reassuring someone about the man who damn near killed Daniel. "Recovery therapy isn't black and white. Matthew will have a therapist and he'll be seeing a doctor and I'm certain he'll also be having daily appointments with a pharmacist. He's in good hands."

Anthony looks at Dan, looks at me, and back to Peter. Satisfied that the rest of us are convinced, he nods. "Thanks, Will. I guess this is difficult for you two to talk about."

Dan and I both shrug at the same time. "It's okay," Dan

says. "I feel so much safer now."

I try to hide my grin behind my cup. The hot chocolate is cold now but whatever.

"You look way better than you did last year," Peter offers, thinking it's a compliment. "I'm so sorry—"

Dan waves his hand, cutting him off. "Please, don't. Все хорошо."

I need to learn.

"Oh," Peter says suddenly. "It was Christmas yesterday, right?"

Grinning again, Dan nods.

"Happy Christmas!"

"Wait, *what*?"

I can't help but laugh at Anthony. "The Orthodox Church has a different calendar to us," I explain. "Advent ends on January sixth."

"You're a Christian?" Anthony asks, one eyebrow raised.

Dan laughs. "Нет," he says. "But I was raised in an ortho-dox family, and it is what I was used to. It was very nice of William to think about it."

"Cas and Lilley thought about it," I say quickly.

Dan shrugs. "You put effort in."

I realise I'm blushing, but I don't bother hiding. I just finish my drink and smile.

"Oh, and you didn't miss anything when you went to New Zealand," Anthony says, nodding. 'Smart."

Dan hums. "I did not think of that."

"Did you have a nice day yesterday?" Peter asks, dragging

the conversation back on track.

"Yes, thank you." Dan's left hand rests very subtly on my thigh. "William spoiled me."

"Hardly," I mutter.

Peter and Anthony obviously think this is adorable. "The teeny tree was very cute," Peter says, folding his free hand under his chin. The other is still holding Anthony's. "You're a romantic sod."

I glare at him before hiding in Dan's neck again.

"It was lovely," Dan says. "Best Christmas ever."

Before I can tell him off for embarrassing me, Cas and Lilley return. They're balancing bags of crisps, sweets, and—mercifully—a bag of red grapes.

"Yep, they're for you," Lilley says, nudging the grapes towards me. "Loser."

I hold my middle finger up to her and open the bag. I'd love to wash them, really, and hesitate before popping one off the branch.

"Один момент," Dan whispers, pushing against me.

I'm slow to realise he's trying to stand up, and a little stunned, I hop to my feet.

He grabs the bag of grapes and disappears through the door to the kitchen of the café.

I stay standing, lost and suspicious, until he comes back.

Lilley groans. "He's so thoughtful I could puke," she mutters.

I'm inclined to agree. Dan's holding the bag of grapes again, but he's also borrowed a plate. I haven't put my glasses back on, so it isn't until he's right beside me that I realise he washed the grapes for me.

He washed them.

I'm clearly exhausted, because this simple, thoughtful act has me reduced to tears. As soon as Dan puts the plate of grapes down, I turn to hide my face in his chest and let myself cry.

Dan tuts and sits down again, bundling me back into his lap. "Silly," he murmurs. "They are only fruit."

I sniff a few times.

"Mind if I translate for him?" Lilley asks.

Dan laughs very softly, trying not to jostle me, and I feel him shake his head.

"This is Will saying, *the fact you went out of your way to make sure I felt happy eating these little grapes means you must love me*. You're looking after him, Dan, and he's not used to that."

He squeezes me tight. "Get used to it," he mutters. "I love you."

Breathless, I kiss his neck. "I love you too."

It feels so good to say.

When I'm no longer overwhelmed, I dry my face on the backs of my hands and smile up at Dan. He looks relieved to see me again and, while the others are talking, kisses me.

It's a gentle *I'm happy to be here* kiss. It's quick, but we smile at each other and share a private moment where we each know we're grateful for the other.

Fourteen

We go to the pub for dinner. The sky is dark by the time we get there and even more snow has stuck, so the paths are buried under a couple of inches of it. Dan doesn't complain, but he walks so close to me I struggle to stay balanced and end up clinging to him for most of the walk. I think this was his plan.

The pub is crowded and warm, and we sit at our usual table with some significant degree of relief. The SU chairs were not comfortable. Sitting beside Dan on the padded bench while the air smells of beer and gravy and my friends chatter as if they haven't spent the last four hours talking non-stop, I could fall asleep. Again.

"What do you want?" Dan asks, leaning so our heads are together.

Honestly...nothing. I want to sleep. I want to curl up in bed with Dan.

"Usual," I mutter. "And please don't freak out if I don't

eat much—"

"I won't."

"I'm so *tired*." I yawn, leaning right into him. "Fucking hell. Five more exams."

"Tomorrow is in the afternoon, yes?"

I nod.

"We'll go to bed as soon as we're home," he whispers, apparently not realising how very special it is to think of my room as our *home*. "I will be okay tonight."

"You can't control that."

"I'm determined."

I laugh and sit up. The others are still deciding what they want to eat, so it doesn't matter that I'm completely ignoring them.

"If you *do* wake up, baby, you've got to wake me too."

Dan pouts at me.

"I mean it."

"I will be fine."

"Yeah, but—"

He kisses me to shut me up. It's so bold, and so confidently *queer* while we sit in this pub full of middle-aged men, that I completely forget how to respond when his lips leave mine and he gets to his feet.

My mouth is still open. I'm still leaning towards where he was sitting.

Peter and Cassie go up to order too, and I'm useless until Lilley kicks me under the table.

"You okay?" she asks. I expected some sly comment. "Is

Dan okay?"

"Yeah, we're both good," I say, and it's the truth. "I'm tired, he's tired. But we're okay."

Lilley purses her lips. "How do you feel about tomorrow?"

I laugh a little loudly. "Honestly, I'm terrified. Shit-scared."

She rolls her eyes. "You smashed today. That's a good sign."

I bite my lip and shrug.

"You'll be *fine.*" She sighs. "This time tomorrow you'll be bouncing off the walls."

I glance at Anthony, hoping he'll change the subject and rescue me. He doesn't.

"If I fail, I'm allowed to blame you lot. Right?"

Lilley snorts. "Sure. Yeah, if you fail tomorrow's exam you can blame me."

Fortunately, Dan comes back to us. He slips his arm around my shoulder before even sitting down and, smug, I cuddle into his chest.

Lilley rolls her eyes.

"Want me to read some questions?" Dan asks, hand out for my phone.

I give it without hesitating.

Lilley starts a conversation with Anthony, which is pretty admirable of her. I know she doesn't like small talk, and I don't know how much she likes Peter's boyfriend. It's not like Anthony has really had a chance to fit into our friendship group yet.

"Okay, darling," Dan begins, opening my notes. "Пять things you are assessed on."

I hold my hand out on the table to count. "History check, physical check, communication, reasoning, and practical."

"Hold up," Lilley says, kicking me again. "Are we revising medicine or Russian?"

I blink at her.

"How many things did you list then?"

Dan kisses my hair and says it again. "Пять."

"And that is...?"

"Five," I answer, surprising myself. "Don't ask how I know."

"You have been listening," Dan whispers.

I'm absolutely *beaming*.

Peter and Cassie come back to us and ask what they've missed.

"They're just being disgusting." Lilley sighs. "As always."

I can't deny it. I just stay happily cuddled under Dan's arm and concentrate when he asks me more questions.

It's difficult to study for a practical exam. I have to do more than prove I know something: I have to prove I can physically do something. I'm nervous, but the things Dan asks me are all second-nature. Answers come easily, and when our dinners are brought over, I'm actually hungry.

No one talks to me while I eat. I'm grateful and, when I put my knife and fork down, the only acknowledgement is Dan putting his arm around my shoulders again.

Okay. I could sleep now.

We stay while everyone else finishes eating, but it's clear, I think, that I'm done for the day. I'm comfortable on this padded seat with Dan's arm around me. I'm warm. I'm fed. I feel safe.

The others order pudding. One-handed, Dan digs the box of gum out of his coat pocket and finds a square. He would *love* to walk back to my room with a cigarette, and the fact he's actively choosing to quit fills me with overwhelming, toe-tingling warmth.

I love him.

He's so, so strong.

"William?" he whispers, making me jump.

Fuck, did I fall asleep *again*?

"Do I need to carry you home?"

"No," I grumble, rubbing the side of my nose. Ouch. "Sorry. You're just so warm."

"You're like a kitten," Cassie says, smiling at me over a spoonful of ice cream. I can't have been out for long if they're all still eating. "Give you a cosy spot and you're gone."

I yawn.

"Are we boring you?" Lilley asks.

"Dan's been keeping him up at night," Peter teases, trying to be funny but accidentally making Dan turn to stone.

I roll my eyes. "Not for *that*."

"Nothing wrong with *that*—"

"No, but we've had a fucking stressful week," I snap. "Not as funny as you thought it was."

Anthony glances at me and nudges my arm very gently. He's apologising, which is really sweet, but I can't look at him without remembering what Dan told me.

Anthony and Matthew—

"Will always needs more sleep in general," Lilley says. "Never have I known anyone so proficient at ignoring their own body's needs."

I raise an eyebrow at her. "I'm sorry, did I miss something? Is this *be rude to Will* day?"

Dan chuckles.

"Prove me wrong," Lilley says, a soft smile spreading across her lips. "Go on. You need your beauty sleep before you diagnose patients tomorrow."

I twist to look up at Dan. He's waiting patiently for me to make a decision, so I nod.

"Fine. They don't want us here anymore," I tease. "Let's go."

"Give me a hug first!" Cas cries, leaping to her feet. I haven't even got my coat on yet, but Dan slides out of the way to let me out.

When I've got my coat done up, Cas throws her arms around me and squeezes me tight.

"So proud of you," she whispers. "You're doing great."

"Only done one exam so far," I mutter. "But thank you."

"Love you." She lets go and sits down again. "Peter won't get up to hug you because he's too busy feeding ice cream to his boyfriend."

"Excuse me?" Peter laughs and puts the spoon back in

the bowl.

On the other side of Cas, Lilley rolls her eyes.

"Never too busy for a hug."

"Could fool me," I say, smiling.

Peter pulls a face, hops to his feet, and shuffles around the table to give me a hug. It's really nice. We hugged on Monday night, but so much has happened over the last few months that we need more than *one* hug—we need time.

I'm happy to give us time.

Hugging Peter makes things feel normal again.

By the time we've said bye to everyone, I've almost woken up. The night air is cold and it makes us both gasp when we step outside, caught by surprise.

"I *will* carry you if I need to," Dan says, but I'm not sure if he means it seriously or not. "Was this evening okay?"

I grin up at him and shove my hands into my pockets, trying to keep warm. Dan still has my pencil case in his pocket, and he keeps one hand out while we walk.

"It was so lovely," I say. "We can't do this after every exam, though."

Dan chuckles and drapes his free arm over my shoulders. I could get used to walking like this.

"Maybe not. But I will be there for you after each one."

My stomach jumps with excitement. "But you have work to do."

Dan just tuts for an answer.

"I'm gonna meet up for revision on Friday morning," I remind him. "Is that okay?"

He squeezes my shoulders. "Of course."

"What will you do?"

He sighs. "I suppose I will find a way to survive for a few hours."

It isn't until I look up and see the way he's smirking that I realise he's teasing.

"I was just asking," I grumble, catching his hand to keep his arm around me. "Are you gonna be at home or on campus?"

"I *do* have studying to do. And I need to talk to Owen about when I'll work this semester."

A grin flashes across my face. I can't help it. Thinking about the short-term future is an absolute thrill: this is what I'm doing this degree for. "I have placements."

"I know you do," Dan says, sounding almost as proud as I feel excited. "I will have to get used to days without you."

I smile up at him. "Yeah. But I'm pretty certain we're going to find a way to spend every night together, aren't we?"

"Oh, probably." He kisses my hair mid-step, taking my breath away. "You can always ask for space."

I squeeze his fingers. "So can you."

For a few moments, we walk through the snow in silence. Our breath clouds around us like smoke and I keep looking up at Dan, hoping he knows how grateful I am for him. I hope he knows how proud I am of all the things he's done—especially over the last few months. I hope he knows how much it means to me that he's quitting smoking.

My stupid comment last night is still weighing on me,

though, and it feels like the perfect time to apologise.

"Dan, about last night—"

"What about it?"

I look up, expecting some sort of irritation or sign he's wary. There's nothing. He looks exactly as he did when he first put his arm around me.

"I'm sorry for what I said," I whisper. "I know it was shit. I shouldn't have talked about drugs like that, and I hope you're not too upset. But I understand if you are."

He sighs and makes us stop walking so we can look at each other without risk of falling. Usually I love this, but right now I'm terrified of what sort of sadness I might see. "Thank you for apologising again," he says, voice soft and calm. "I know you didn't mean to upset me."

"But then I *did*. I was horrible."

He raises an eyebrow. "It was insensitive, but I understand what you meant."

I grimace.

"I, of all people, should understand the benefit of taking replacement drugs—I *understand*," he whispers. His right hand comes up to touch my chin. "You have time to work on your bedside manner before you are with patients."

I blush horrendously. "Not really. I start in February."

Dan winks at me and leans down so the tip of his nose is almost against mine. "Time."

I roll my eyes, but he's right. I'm never going to make that mistake again and, even though I was *technically* right, did it help Dan? I don't think so.

So I file this away, along with when I tried to tell Dan I was *proud* of him for his background, and call it a learning moment. I went wrong. I messed up.

Dan kisses my cheek very lightly and stands up again, taking my hand. "Let's keep going," he says. "You need sleep."

I shrug, but I follow his lead and keep walking. The path is slippery with slush and I keep splashing in puddles which are deeper than I expect, so my feet are going to be soaked by the time we get home. Gross.

"I had an idea," he says.

I wait patiently to hear the rest, but Dan keeps his eyes forward. He's nervous.

"Lilley thought it was good."

"She'll always be honest with you," I say, confident in *that*, at least. My stomach is doing nervous flutters. "What's this idea?"

He hesitates. I'm not used to seeing him doubt himself like this. If Dan wants to do something, he does it. What could be so scary that he can't tell me?

We've been through everything together.

I wait. I keep holding his hand, rubbing his cold fingers and letting him gather his thoughts. Maybe he's changed his mind about telling me. Maybe he'd rather tell me when Lilley's with us—

"I could apply for a master's," he whispers.

The path we're walking along becomes steeper here, as we descend one of the many hills at Keele. It's slippery and dangerous in the snow, so he unhooks his arm from my shoulder. I catch his hand again and take a breath before responding.

"What would you want to do?"

I want to scream. I want to leap at him and kiss him, because a master's means another year with us guaranteed to be in the same country, but he's nervous. I need to be gentle. No more mistakes.

"We have an international diplomacy MSc." He still won't look at me. "It would lead on from politics. And you can study a language with it."

I laugh. "You need *another* language?"

"I would like a certificate in something other than English," he says, finally turning his head to wink at me. Goodness me. "I could formalise Spanish."

My heart leaps. "You'd like that, wouldn't you?"

"*And* I would have a better chance at getting a job here," he says quickly. "It is not just the languages."

"No, but you could actually use them." A sad thought hits me, and I make us stop walking. "Dan, your Spanish heritage doesn't need a certificate to be real. You know that, right?"

He rolls his eyes, but he's blushing. "I know."

"Convince me, Dan."

With a tiny, self-conscious laugh, he leans down and kisses my cheek. I can feel his warm breath. "Lo se gracias."

It's a good start. "We can find exams for you to sit in Spanish," I say. "But wouldn't you get bored learning it from scratch?"

Still with his face by mine, he hums. "It would be like

having free time."

I laugh and grab him for a hug. His coat is cold. "It would. You can think about it, right? There's no rush."

"No rush."

"What other languages do they offer?" I don't want to be pushy here, but learning his mother's language with a room full of complete beginners feels like it could be a waste of time.

He sighs and steps back, out of my arms. "Russian."

I raise an eyebrow and wait for more.

"German could be interesting. Mandarin and Japanese— but would either of those be more useful than Russian?"

"Would you be *interested* in them?" I ask, pushing my hair back with one hand. "That's what matters. Or—what would be your real motivation for learning another language? The opportunities it might bring?"

He shrugs. "I think so."

"Okay. Maybe this is something you could talk to someone at the language centre about." I take his hand. We've been apart for long enough, thanks. "The really important thing is whether you'd enjoy international diplomacy."

"Oh, да," he says, without missing a beat. "I would love it. But it might mean I end up travelling for my job."

"As long as that travelling brings you back to me every now and then." I wink up at him and we start walking again. "That sounds great, Dan. I'm glad you've found something you want to do."

"Thank you," he says it quietly, like he's embarrassed. Maybe he is.

I let us walk past the SU and the library in silence, but this is such an exciting moment for Dan. He's considering his future—and seriously, rather than just vaguely hoping he'll make it through the night. He's thinking about his education as a route to a career, rather than just a reason to stay in England.

I'm so proud of him I could burst. "Dan?"

"Привет."

I'm grinning so much it hurts. "I love you."

He brings my hand up to his lips to kiss. "I love you too," he whispers. "This is a good week."

"It is." Did I just jinx it? "So far."

Dan laughs and shakes his head. "It *is* good."

My accommodation building looms into view, highlighted by orange streetlights and looking grey and uninviting in the snow. Dan hasn't complained about being cold since—

Since Peter mentioned it.

I could scream.

"We'll definitely get you some gloves," I say, digging in my pocket for my key. "Maybe some of those reusable hand warmers."

Dan laughs, sounding sweet and light in the cool air. Good.

"Maybe we should go to Spain one day," I blurt. "Get you some sunshine, give you the chance to show off."

He laughs even more. "Don't tempt me," he warns. "Flights will be booked."

The thrill of excitement I feel at this is a *bad idea*. When am I going to have a chance to jet off to Spain for a holiday? I have the next couple of weeks full of exams, then placements, then more exams—

"You will need to take a break at some point this year," he reminds me. "It could just be a couple of days."

He really, really likes this idea. And I don't blame him. Yes, he's only just got back from New Zealand—but he's had a hell of a time since landing in England. The Easter break is in just a couple of months, and I'm quietly confident he'll take the opportunity to go on holiday. I'm also quietly sad that I know I won't go with him. No matter how lovely a long weekend in Spain with Dan feels, it's just not something I can let myself do at this point in my degree.

Dan notices my shift in mood. I let us into my building and we walk in silence down the corridor to my room.

"I hope you realise the only place I'm going without you is Russia, and that is because I *have* to," Dan says, taking off his coat and handing me my pencil case.

I take it with a timid smile. "*And* wherever you end up going when you work in international diplomacy."

Dan rolls his eyes and catches my face between his newly free hands.

I toss my pencil case half-heartedly towards the floor near my wardrobe, where it might not get stepped on.

"But you will be saving lives by then," he whispers, thumbs stroking across my cheeks to my hairline. "You won't miss me."

"Stupid. Of course I will."

He kisses my forehead. His lips are cold.

"But I'll also be *very* fucking proud of you."

He hums and pushes his face into my hair, hands sliding so they meet behind my head. My eyes close and I take gentle handfuls of his jumper, holding him close but giving us both space to breathe.

"I am always proud of you," he whispers. "And so grateful to be in your life."

I should have taken my glasses off. They're in the way and the only reason, really, that I don't tilt my face up and start kissing his neck.

"I love you, Dan."

He slides one of his hands down my neck and back to cup my waist. My heart trembles, anticipating what's coming, and I struggle to keep my breathing sounding normal. Dan takes his face out of my hair, smiles at me, and...

Lets go of me.

I take an obviously deep breath and hang my coat up, trying to look less flustered than I am. Every time he holds me like that, I feel like I'm the only guy in the world. I forget how worried I am about Dan because a moment in his arms is the closest to peaceful I have ever felt. With his arms around me, he tells me it's okay to feel like I feel—whether that's being desperately in love with him, hesitant about coming out, or stressed about exams—and gives me something safe and good to hold on to.

We get ready for bed, moving together like the pieces of the same unit we've built over the last few months. We take it in turns to brush our teeth at the little washbasin in the corner of my room, Dan takes his prescription, and when we're finally settled together in the cosy, single bed, he speaks again.

"Я тебя люблю," Dan whispers.

I close my eyes and rest my hand on his hip. He's warm, like he should be, and I take a deep breath. It tastes of him.

"Maybe I should see if I can fit that Russian course into my timetable," I murmur. I'm already determined to find some tutorials to help me learn. "It's gonna get embarrassing *fast* if I can't speak to you in your first language while you're off learning your sixth."

Dan chuckles, soft and quiet, and kisses my forehead. "I can help you."

"You can," I agree, "but it's not your job. You just keep chattering to me and I'll do the work."

He presses his face into my hair, accepting this.

My skin floods with warmth as I think about just how much I would love to be able to understand Russian. Maybe we could visit Russia together. We'd be careful, of course, but it could solve the biggest issue with his VISA: the uncertainty. If I could be with him while he navigated loopholes and forms, it wouldn't matter if it took months and months.

Not this side of my degree, though. I wonder if it would be possible for me to do placements somewhere in Russia. Could I do a semester at a university over there, instead of at Keele?

The timeline sketches out in my mind, clearer and more defined than yesterday morning. Dan graduates his undergrad this year (I refuse to consider what happens if he fails). He leaves me for a handful of weeks while he sorts his VISA to continue studying at a master's level. For a year, he studies international diplomacy with Spanish. Or with German. Or with Japanese. I study Russian in every spare moment, more often than not with Dan as my tutor. He graduates again and I enter my fourth year, which is full of placements and exams. If he can't get a job and VISA right away, we both go to Russia and I do my placements there. He gets a job and a VISA, I come back to Keele for my final year, and we live happily ever after.

With his arm still around my back, Dan turns to lie on his front and settles down. There are a lot of *if*s and *maybe*s in this plan, but I think it could work. I'm determined it will work.

"Hey, Dan?"

He hums.

"I'm gonna learn Russian. But maybe I should try Spanish first. I already know *some*—what do you think?"

Dan takes a slow, deep breath and we both wriggle to look at each other. Until we make eye contact, my motives have been entirely selfish.

But shit. I just realised how completely opposite to Matthew it is for me to actively be encouraging Dan to speak in Russian—never mind saying I want to learn his mother's language too. It makes me so angry, but the anger is easily ignored by how happy Dan looks right at this moment.

"Спасибо," he whispers.

Don't cry.

"Thanks for looking after me today," I add. "And for being so nice to Anthony, even though you don't need to, and for not going to Matthew—"

He kisses me.

"We look after each other," he says, when I'm busy blinking stars and love hearts from my eyes. "None of this is Anthony's fault. And I do not want to be near Matthew."

Do not cry.

"Proud of you," I say, voice choked with the threat of tears. Damn it. "I'm always so proud of you."

Dan chuckles and touches the tip of his nose to mine. "Thank you."

What, no argument? No *you can't be proud of me*? I melt right into the mattress and take a twisted handful of his t-shirt.

"Go to sleep, William. I'm okay."

I believe him. We'll discuss my plan for the next couple of years tomorrow, maybe while having breakfast. Maybe while walking in the snow.

I let out a long, tired breath and close my eyes. "Fine. Night, Dan."

He kisses my cheek. "Спокойной ночи."

A note from the author

Not Quite Out finishes on January 5th. Christmas is celebrated on January 6th in Russia. Cas and Lilley didn't make that up.

When I first wrote Marshmallows, *I had no idea what I was going to do with it.*

But here it is!

If you're here because you fell as much in love with Will and Dan as I have, I hope these few pages gave you something similar to that chest-warmth when you take the first sip of hot chocolate after stepping in from the snow. I hope you smiled every time Dan said something in a language other than English. I hope you sighed in relief when Will suggested they get snacks.

Both Will and Dan are going through a lot in this, which I've been fondly referring to as my "fluff novella." Quitting smoking? Not as easy as the adverts make it look. Telling your abusive ex to leave you alone? Difficult, especially when you've already done it before. Second year medicine exams? Brutal.

Being 'out' in public? Scary. Today I wore a rainbow mask while on my own for the first time, and I saw people look at me, then look again. I hope you forgive Will for calling Dan his "friend."

Here's a list of charities which help with some of the themes I've covered across Will and Dan's story with descriptions directly from the charity websites.

The Abortion Support Network: *provides advice on travelling for abortion, financial assistance towards the costs, and, where needed and where possible, accommodation in volunteer homes.*

Planned Parenthood: *delivers vital reproductive health care, sex education, and information to millions of people worldwide.*

AllOut: *mobilizing thousands of people to build a world where no person will have to sacrifice their family or freedom, safety or dignity, because of who they are or who they love.*

BEAT*: the UK's eating disorder charity. Founded in 1989 as the Eating Disorders Association, our mission is to end the pain and suffering caused by eating disorders.*

Galop: *the UK's LGBT+ anti-abuse charity. We work with* *and for LGBT+ victims and survivors of interpersonal abuse and violence.*

MindOut: *a mental health service run by and for lesbians, gay, bisexual, trans and queer people with experience of mental health issues.*

Acknowledgements

I'd like to thank the fantastic people I've met through Twitter who, perhaps unintentionally, encouraged me to keep writing this fluff novella. If we've ever shared DMs about Dan and Will it was your enthusiasm that kept me going. Thank you for the writing sprints, the AMAs, the giveaways, the general enthusiasm and the friendship.

I'd like to special-shout-out the wonderful team at Queer Lit, who supported me before I even knew I needed support. I've learned a lot from you.

D, Ellie, Jess: goodness me, you've kept me going through yet another book release. Thank you. I love the bunch of you. Lunch date soon?

Rue: I am honored to have a book graced with your artwork. I'm so grateful for your friendship and support— you inspire me at every turn.

I want to list my twitter friends, but I'm terrified of missing someone. Y'all know who you are. I couldn't have done this without you.

The team at Lost Boys Press: thank you for loving Dan

and Will almost as much as I do, and for supporting me through this publishing journey.

Everyone who contacted me specifically to say something positive about Not Quite Out*: you have no idea how wonderful it was to hear from you. Whether it was to say you identified with Will or hated him, you made him feel like a real person who existed beyond just my own imagination. That's magic.*

Please stay safe and continue to take care of yourself. We all need each other.

About the author

Louise Willingham is a geographer and writer whose interests range from forensics to plant care and most things in between. She published her debut novel, Not Quite Out, *in 2021 and has been using the leftover promotional materials to raise money for the Abortion Support Network.*

Lightning Source UK Ltd.
Milton Keynes UK
UKHW022305281222
414536UK00009B/103